"Daddy, you're at Miss Melanie."

Rebecca grabbed her teddy bear and buried her face to stifle the laughter.

Jackson and Melanie broke out laughing.

"I was not." He examined Melanie more closely. "Was I?" He winked and slammed the passenger door shut.

"Can Miss Melanie come with us to the apple festival?"

"Well, that's up to Miss Melanie."

Rebecca jumped up and down. "Please, will you come with us?"

"Yes, please." He plucked a brilliant red wildflower and handed it to Melanie.

She brought it to her nose. "Ah…it smells so good. And yes, I'd love to go with you."

Rebecca skipped down the dirt path.

Melanie smelled the flower again as she gazed at Rebecca.

Jackson took a deep breath. "I think there's nothing more beautiful than you holding that wildflower."

He saw the color bloom on her cheeks.

Jackson couldn't resist any longer…she was getting into his heart.

Weekdays, **Jill Weatherholt** works for the City of Charlotte. On the weekend, she writes contemporary stories about love, faith and forgiveness. Raised in the suburbs of Washington, DC, she now resides in North Carolina. She holds a degree in psychology from George Mason University and a paralegal studies certification from Duke University. She shares her life with her real-life hero and number one supporter. Jill loves connecting with readers at jillweatherholt.com.

Books by Jill Weatherholt

Love Inspired

Second Chance Romance

Second Chance Romance

Jill Weatherholt

HARLEQUIN® LOVE INSPIRED®

Recycling programs
for this product may
not exist in your area.

LOVE INSPIRED BOOKS

ISBN-13: 978-0-373-89919-7

Second Chance Romance

Copyright © 2017 by Jill Weatherholt

www.Harlequin.com

Printed in U.S.A.

Trust in the Lord with all your heart
and lean not on your own understanding;
in all your ways submit to Him,
and He will make your paths straight.
—*Proverbs* 3:5–6

To Derek, thank you for all of your patience and encouragement. You're my number one cheerleader. And to my mother, father and my sister, Jan, who've given me a lifetime of support.

Chapter One

"Miss, can you hear me?" Jackson's chest tightened. "C-can you open the door?"

The rain hitting his face felt like acupuncture needles. "I'm Jackson Daughtry, a paramedic. Can you hear me?"

The woman inside the silver Volvo didn't respond. Her body slumped over the steering wheel, but he could tell she was breathing. Her flowing chestnut curls were covered in blood. He gripped the driver's side door. It didn't budge. He beat on the window. His knuckles burned.

"Hold on, miss." It was Thursday, his first day off in ten days. Thankfully he was always prepared. Inside his trunk, he kept a fully stocked first-aid kit with compress dressings and bandages, all of the proper supplies for an emergency. "I'll have you out before you open your eyes. You'll be fine."

Mud tried to tug his boots from his feet while he sprinted to his truck. Inside his Bronco, he wiped the pellets of rain off his face and grabbed his phone to call the station.

"Tom, it's Jackson. I'm on Smith Farm Road, in front of the old Smith farm. I need an ambulance."

"I thought today was your day off."

"I was on my way to pick up Rebecca from the Whitesides' house. She spent the night with her friend Mary." He paused to catch his breath. "A deer darted across the road, and the car in front of me swerved straight into a chestnut oak. The driver is bleeding from her head, and she's unconscious. Can you send the ambulance and contact the sheriff? I'll make the report at the hospital."

"Sorry, bud—I'll call the sheriff, but the ambulance is at the Swanson place. They think Betsy had a heart attack. Poor Walter, he was beside himself when he called. Betsy collapsed while taking the roast out of the oven. It'll be a while."

Jackson's stomach churned. The only downside of living in the small mountain valley of Sweet Gum, Virginia, was that there was only one sheriff's car and one ambulance. "Call over to Waynesboro. They'll send one."

"No can do, my friend. I heard over the radio there's a bad accident on Route 340."

Jackson straightened his shoulders. "Never mind. I'll take her to Sweet Gum Memorial myself." He clenched his teeth, causing a pain to shoot through his jaw.

"Who is she, Jackson? Should I call her family?"

"She's unconscious, man, and the car's locked." He massaged his temples. His head pounded. "The license plate says Washington, DC." He remembered Rebecca, his precious daughter. "Do you mind calling over to the Whitesides' house? Tell them I'll be there as soon as I can."

"Consider it done."

Jackson pressed End. He grabbed the slim jim from his trunk, but it slipped from his hands and sank into the mud. He yanked it loose and sprinted to the Volvo. He jammed it down into the crack between the door and the window. Nothing happened. The car was a newer model. The slim jim wasn't going to get him inside. He raced back to his trunk and grabbed a tire iron. He had no choice.

Standing next to the passenger window, he took a swing, and the glass exploded. With ease, he reached inside, popped the lock and flung open the door.

"You'll be fine." *Please, Lord, let her be okay.* "I'm going to unbuckle your seat belt and lift you out," he told her, though she was still out cold.

The seat belt was stubborn. His knuckles throbbed from pounding on the window. "Hold on. I can't get my hands on the release. One second and I'll have you out." Finally free, Jackson closed his eyes for an instant and tore off his bomber jacket.

"This will keep you warm and toasty." He covered her with his leather jacket. Despite her slender frame, maneuvering her from behind the steering wheel wasn't an easy task. His boots slid in the mud, and his knee rammed against the side of the Volvo. Rain pelted his face, stinging like sleet. He shivered when he glanced at the sky. It was dark as ink. *Please, Lord, help me get her free.* With precise movements he'd learned at the training academy and an answered prayer, finally she was in his arms.

She was featherlight. He carried her to the truck and laid her in the backseat as though she were made of antique china. "Let's make sure you're nice and comfortable," he said, with hopes that his voice would somehow gradually bring her out of her unconscious state.

He scanned her face and pushed away a strand of blood-soaked hair. There were serious cuts on her cheek and forehead.

He dashed to the car to get her purse. Then he jerked open the passenger side door and spied a piece of paper on the floor. Drops of rain trickled down his hands when he picked it up. The ink had smeared, but it was still legible, and he could see it was directions to Phoebe Austin's farm. He snatched the purse and bolted to his truck. He'd call Phoebe once he arrived at the hospital.

Inside the truck, he jerked the seat belt over his shoulder, turned and slid his phone from his shirt pocket. "Hold on. I'm going to get you to the hospital as fast as I can, but first I have to call to tell them we're on our way." Never one for high-tech gadgets, he opened his old flip phone. With the hospital on speed dial, he punched number nine. He tapped his foot while he waited for an answer.

After three rings, he heard a familiar voice. "Sweet Gum Memorial. This is Sara."

He gulped in a deep breath. "Sara…hi. I'm glad you're working. It's Jackson." He often had to dodge her advances, but she was a good nurse. He trusted her skills.

After giving her details of the accident, and their estimated time of arrival, he hit End and tossed his phone on the passenger seat. He gripped the steering wheel and closed his eyes. *Lord, please watch over this woman. Guide us as we travel in these dangerous conditions.*

Jackson started up the car, then jammed his foot on the accelerator and turned on the windshield wipers. The windows fogged. He rubbed his hand in large circles along the front windshield. He'd meant to get the defroster checked. There was never enough time.

"Are you okay back there?" He knew she wouldn't answer, but maybe she could hear his words. "So, you were on your way to Phoebe's house? She's quite a character, isn't she? We own a business together, The Coffee Bean. She runs the place. I'm just a backup, if she needs help. Did she tell you?" He blew out a breath. *Lord, please, let her answer me.*

The ride seemed endless. The pounding rain knocked the red maple leaves from the trees, splattering onto his windshield and littering the winding two-lane road. Deer grazed in a field, oblivious to the deluge. He eased his foot off the accelerator when his truck hydroplaned for a second time. "No sense in having another accident." Up ahead a tree toppled over, thankfully not onto the road. He bit his lip. If only she would answer.

At last, through the foggy window, he spied

the red glow of the emergency-room entrance. *Thank You, Lord, for getting us here safe.* Within seconds, Steve, a tall and lanky orderly, rushed toward his truck, pushing a gurney.

Jackson's chest expanded. He unbuckled his seat belt and shot from the truck. "Hey, Steve. How's it going?"

"Busy. This storm is creating lots of problems," Steve said while he and Jackson removed the victim out of the truck and onto the gurney. "Has she been unconscious since you found her?"

Jackson wiped his hands down the front of his jeans. The rain tapered to a light drizzle. "Yes, she was out cold when I got inside her car."

"Dr. Roberts is on duty," Steve noted as he covered her with a blanket and pushed the rolling bed toward the hospital.

"That's good." Jackson turned and climbed into his truck. "I'm going to park. I'll be right in."

Inside the ER, Jackson approached Nurse Sara. With a clipboard in hand, she scribbled something with a red pen. She stopped and looked up. "Hi, Jackson. I'm glad you made it safe. Steve took the victim back to see the doctor." She winked and flashed an overly whitened smile. "Did you find out her name?"

He handed her the purse he'd retrieved from

the scene of the accident. "I don't feel comfortable going through a woman's things. You go ahead and check out her driver's license."

She took the bag and dumped its contents onto the counter. "Here it is. Her name is Melanie Harper."

He arched an eyebrow. "I don't know of any Harper in the area, do you?"

"I can't think of any."

Sara made it her business to know everyone's business. If she said there weren't any Harpers in these parts, there weren't.

"According to the license, she has a Washington, DC, address." Sara tucked a strand of hair behind her ear. "You said you found directions to Phoebe's house inside her car. That must be where she was going." She scooped the contents back into the purse.

He reached for his phone. "I'm going to step outside and call Phoebe. If Dr. Roberts comes out, tell him I'll be right back." He headed toward the back entrance and prayed Phoebe was either at The Coffee Bean or at home. Just like him, she wasn't a fan of tech gadgets. She didn't even own a cell phone, which made it difficult to reach her sometimes.

Outside, the storm had passed, and a glimpse of the sun slipped between the drifting clouds. Autumn in the valley was his favorite time of the year. He hit the number two on his phone and took a seat on the only dry bench in the courtyard. It was under a roof, but the warmth of the sun tapped his face. He glanced at his watch and saw it was 12:30 p.m. Since The Bean's first day, his mother and Phoebe had made the decision to open only for breakfast and lunch. He hoped the afternoon crowd was winding down so Phoebe would pick up.

"The Coffee Bean. This is Phoebe."

Phoebe's voice always brought a smile to his face. After his parents' deaths, she'd been like a mother to him and a grandmother to his daughter, Rebecca. His mother and Phoebe had grown up together and had opened The Coffee Bean as co-owners. When his mother had died only a year after his father, she'd left her ownership to Jackson. Over the years, he remained a silent partner, since Phoebe wanted to run the show on her own.

"Phoebe, it's Jackson."

"Well, hello there, Mr. Daughtry."

No matter her circumstances, Phoebe was always full of joy. Jackson loved that about her. "Were you expecting company today?" The last thing in the world he wanted to do was cause Phoebe pain, but he had to tell her about Melanie.

"Yes, my niece, Melanie," she answered.

"You've heard me speak of her." Dishes clanked in the background. "She's the successful divorce attorney from Washington, DC. The one who never takes a vacation."

He remembered. Phoebe had tried to convince her niece to visit Sweet Gum for years, but she'd always been too busy. He knew that she'd made partner at her law firm at an unusually young age. He thought she had a family, but maybe he was wrong. Something had happened last year, but Phoebe never wanted to talk about it. He wasn't the type to get into people's business, so he'd never pursued the subject.

"Jackson? Are you there? Is everything okay?"

His chest felt heavy. "It's Melanie." He gazed across the courtyard. A squirrel scurried through the fescue, toting a nut in its mouth.

"Melanie?" The dishes stopped clanking. "What happened?"

Jackson knew Phoebe better than most, but he wasn't quite sure how she would react to the news. "She's been in a car accident." He paused to give her time to take in the news.

"Oh my word! Is she okay?" Phoebe asked, releasing short breaths into the phone.

"She was unconscious when I pulled her from the car."

"Unconscious!"

"Please calm down and let me finish. There's a serious cut on her forehead and one on her cheek. Though I don't know if she has any internal injuries or a concussion. She's in the ER with Dr. Roberts."

"Thank God he's on duty. He's the best. I'll be there as fast as I can."

"Why don't you stay put? I'll pick you up. You shouldn't drive when you're upset."

There was no hesitation. "Don't be ridiculous. It will take longer. Besides, I want you there with Melanie until I arrive."

He'd learned years ago not to argue with her. "Please take your time. The rain has stopped, but the roads are covered in wet leaves. It's very slick. Be safe."

"Don't worry. I've been driving these roads since I was a teenager." Phoebe hung up without saying goodbye.

Jackson turned and walked inside the hospital. He hoped to get a little information on Melanie's condition from Sara, but he'd probably need to wait for Phoebe so they could both talk to Dr. Roberts.

Once inside, cleaning agents infiltrated his nose. He spied Sara chatting with a handsome young doctor. Jackson took a seat in the waiting room and prayed for the next ten minutes.

Finally Sara walked toward him. He stood

and met her halfway. She brushed her blond bangs away from her eyes. "Dr. Roberts is ready to speak with Phoebe when she arrives."

Jackson ran his hand across his chin. It was rough. He never liked to shave on his days off. One fewer thing to do. "How's Melanie? Has she regained consciousness?"

Sara pursed her lips. "I'm sorry, Jackson, but you know I can't talk to you about her condition. Neither can Dr. Roberts. You'll have to wait for Phoebe."

The young nurse disappeared through the ER doors, leaving behind a trail of potent fragrance.

Within a couple of minutes, Dr. Roberts appeared. Jackson had always admired him. With salt-and-pepper hair and slightly slumped shoulders, his experience was evident in his face and manner of speaking. He still worked five days a week and even made the occasional house call, if needed. He'd been on the staff at Sweet Gum Memorial for decades. He was not only an excellent doctor but also a pillar within the community.

"Dr. Roberts, it's good to see you." Jackson rubbed his hand across the back of his neck. Another tension headache was setting in.

The doctor smiled and extended his hand. "It's good to see you, too, Jackson. It's been a while. How's your sweet little girl?"

Jackson shook his offered hand. "She's great. Thanks for asking. This year she started afternoon kindergarten. She's a voracious reader."

Dr. Roberts nodded. "That's great to hear. Books can open up an entire world to a child." He cleared his throat. "Now, back to the patient. You know the confidentiality laws prohibit me from talking to you about Melanie's condition. Once Phoebe arrives, I'll fill you both in if it's okay with Phoebe. She's next of kin, so she'll make the call. I know you're worried, so I'll say only that you can relax."

"That makes me feel better." Although she was just a stranger, there was something about Melanie. He wanted to protect her. He wasn't sure where these feelings were coming from. Maybe it was because of her relationship to Phoebe. What else could it be?

"Speaking of Phoebe, how is she doing these days?"

Jackson noticed a sparkle in Dr. Roberts's eye when he asked about Phoebe. Many years had passed since Phoebe's husband had died. Jackson always hoped for a spark to ignite between her and the doctor. He'd love to see her enjoy a little male companionship. She still had many years ahead of her, time she shouldn't spend alone. Of course, people could have said the same thing about him. "Phoebe's doing great, busy as ever. I called her about fifteen minutes ago. I told her I'd pick her up since the roads are so treacherous. Of course she insisted on driving herself."

He smiled. "Sure sounds like Phoebe. She's quite stubborn when she gets her mind set on something. I'll never forget that after my sweet Jane went to be with the Lord, Phoebe brought me an enormous meal every day. I told her it wasn't necessary, but she insisted. I had mashed potatoes coming out of my ears." Dr. Roberts laughed a deep belly laugh.

Jackson thought now was the time to slip in a good word about Phoebe, and perhaps devise a plan of action. "She's stubborn, but you have to admit she's a terrific cook. Her meat loaf and garlic mashed potatoes are the best in the valley." He'd always heard people say the way to a man's heart was through his stomach. "You should taste her new apple-pie recipe. She puts in just the right amount of cinnamon."

"Stop, Jackson. You're making me ravenous." His tongue ran across his lips, and he rubbed his stomach. "I haven't had time to eat lunch. I'll probably have a slice or two of frozen pizza for dinner."

Perhaps overstepping his bounds, Jackson took a chance. This man needed a home-cooked meal and a little female companionship.

"I should talk to Phoebe about inviting you over for Sunday dinner. She always cooks enough for an army. Rebecca and I come home with a ton of leftovers." Phoebe loved to have a house full of people. He'd definitely work on this.

Dr. Roberts nodded. "I like the way you think, young man. Just tell me when and I'll be there." He extended his hand to Jackson. "I'll come out and talk to Phoebe when she arrives. Oh, and make sure she introduces you to Melanie. I'm sure she'd love to meet the man who rescued her."

"Thanks again," Jackson said and took a seat to wait for Phoebe's arrival.

When she burst through the hospital entrance minutes later, he saw her quickly race down the hall straight toward him. "How is she, Jackson?" She removed her raincoat and flung it over her arm.

Sara came down the hallway holding a cup of coffee in each hand. "Hi, Phoebe. I saw you pull into the parking lot. I'm happy you made it here safe." She smiled. "I thought you and Jackson could use this." She handed them each a steaming Styrofoam cup. "I'll let Dr. Roberts know you're here." She pointed to a private room next to the waiting area. "You can have a seat in there."

Jackson nodded and took a quick sip. Strong

and black, it was just what he needed. "Thanks for the coffee, Sara." He took hold of Phoebe's hand. "Let's go sit down for a minute."

A small circular oak table and four chairs filled the entire windowless room. The strong aroma of the cleaning agents in the hallway gave way to the smell of pink tea roses in a crystal vase decorating the middle of the table. The chair screeched when Jackson pulled it out for Phoebe.

"Melanie's going to be fine." He reached across the table, placing his hand on hers. "I don't want you to worry."

They prayed quietly until Dr. Roberts, clipboard in hand, joined them. He took a seat and smiled. "Hello, Phoebe. It's good to see you."

"It's nice to see you, too. How's Melanie?"

"She's as strong as they come. She regained consciousness shortly after Jackson brought her in. Her memory appears fine, so that's a blessing. The X-rays are all clear, no broken bones. But the MRI showed she does have a slight concussion, so we'll keep her overnight, but she'll be ready to go home with you in the morning."

Phoebe clapped her hands together. "Thank God! The poor girl has been through enough." She released a heavy breath. "Thank you so much, Doctor."

Jackson considered Phoebe's statement. Melanie must have endured some type of hardship, but now was not the time to ask questions. He squeezed the older woman's hand. "Let's stay focused on the positive."

Dr. Roberts left, and they stood under the flickering fluorescent lights in silence. Phoebe stepped forward. "One day you're going to make another woman very happy, Mr. Daughtry. Now let's go check on my niece. I can't wait for the two of you to meet."

Jackson nodded. As they walked down the hall toward Melanie's room, his breath quickened. At the doorway, he closed his eyes for a moment and took a calming breath. Why was he so nervous? He felt like a teenage boy getting ready for his first date.

Melanie opened her eyes, but quickly closed them again to escape the searing pain. The fluorescent lights burned her vision. Who in the world invented fluorescent lighting, anyway? It was the worst.

Images flashed through her mind of a whitetail deer tearing across the road, her car headed toward a tree, and then everything went black.

She opened her eyes again to see a woman's face peering through a curtain.

Hospital. She should have known. Hospitals always had annoying fluorescent lights.

"How's our patient feeling?" asked a petite blonde woman carrying a frosted pitcher and a plastic cup. She approached the bedside and smiled.

Stiff.

Exactly how Melanie had felt after she completed her fifth marathon, one month before her life had changed forever. She squirmed in an attempt to sit up, but a pain shot down her neck, like needles jabbing into her skin. She nestled back under the sheet.

"I'm Sara, your nurse." She filled the cup with water and pulled a red straw from her pocket. "Try to drink a little. You need to stay hydrated."

Melanie took the cup and placed the straw to her parched lips. "Is my aunt Phoebe here?" She sipped the cool liquid and flinched when it touched the back of her throat. "I remember a deer running in front of my car. Is that why I'm here?" She pressed her palm to her forehead. Her head throbbed as though someone bashed a rubber hammer against it.

"Here, take this. It will help with the pain, but it will make you sleepy."

Melanie reached for the tiny clear cup that held the medicine as the nurse walked toward the window and tilted the blinds. "I've always preferred natural light." She flipped a switch, and the fluorescent beacon vanished.

The pressure in Melanie's head and around her eyes eased. "Thank you so much. I love the natural light, too." She took another sip of the water, ran her fingers down the side of the cup and glanced out the window. "It stopped raining." She wiped her fingers, wet from the moisture, onto her gown. "Can you tell me what happened?"

Sara placed her fist under her chin. Her fingernails were painted bloodred. "From what I understand, Jackson—"

"Jackson? Who's Jackson?"

Sara flashed a mischievous smile. "Why, he's the most handsome paramedic in all of Sweet Gum Valley, honey. Every woman within a hundred-mile radius would love to lasso the charming Mr. Daughtry, myself included." She smoothed the back of her hair and placed her right hand across her narrow hip. "He's the person who rescued you."

Details were a blur, with the exception of the blinding rain, the deer and a tree. "Rescued me?" There were many events over the last year that she'd love to forget, but this wasn't one of them. "Please, tell me what happened."

"You were in a car accident on Smith Farm Road. Jackson was in the car behind you. He saw the deer dart across the road. You swerved to miss it and hit a tree." Sara reached down and brushed a strand of hair away from Melanie's face. "By the look of those cuts on your cheek and forehead, God was watching over you."

Melanie put her hand to her forehead. *He's forgotten about me.*

The white walls of the tiny room closed in around her. Why had she left DC? She wanted to go home and back to the job that occupied her mind for more than seventy hours a week—sometimes more. Work erased the pain of the past year.

When Aunt Phoebe had called last week and begged her to come for a visit, Melanie had finally given in. Phoebe was Melanie's only living relative. She hoped to convince Phoebe to move to DC and live with her. Aunt Phoebe was her father's younger sister. Somewhere in her attic, probably stuck in a box and gathering dust, Melanie had a photo of them together as children. She released a heavy breath. "I want to see my aunt Phoebe. Is she here?"

"Yes, Phoebe's here. She's down the hall, talking with Jackson."

Sara headed toward the door and turned. "I'll be at the nurses' station. Push the button if you need anything, sweetie."

Melanie rested her head against the mountain

of pillows, mindlessly staring at the ceiling. She wished she could disappear through a crack in the drywall and go back to her home in DC.

Moments later she heard footsteps in the hall. They stopped outside the door, and there was a gentle knock. "Can we come in?"

Melanie gave the sheet a slight tug to cover her flimsy blue hospital gown. "Yes." The sight of Aunt Phoebe's smiling face in the doorway brought tears to Melanie's eyes. The last time they'd seen each other had been the funeral. Had it really been a year? Some days it felt like an eternity.

"Oh dear, thank God you're okay." Aunt Phoebe glided across the floor to her bedside and kissed her forehead. "I was so worried about you. I don't know what would have happened if Jackson hadn't been there. Your car was towed to Wilbourn's Autobody, so no need to fret about that. It will be repaired in a couple of days."

Her aunt turned toward the door, and Melanie's eyes followed. Her breath caught in her throat. A gorgeous, tall man with dark, wavy hair and a muscular frame stood in the doorway.

Their eyes connected for an instant, and her heart fluttered when his cheeks flushed. "I suppose you're the infamous Jackson." When he smiled, she looked away, but not before she took notice of his hypnotic deep blue eyes. He was perfection—which was reason enough to avoid him.

"Come in, Jackson." Aunt Phoebe beamed and extended her hand toward him. "I'd like to introduce you to my lovely niece." She moved aside, and he sauntered toward Melanie's bed with his thumbs through his belt loops. "Jackson Daughtry, this is my niece, Melanie Harper."

Jackson jerked his thumbs loose and touched his hand to hers. She expected roughness. The silky smooth feel of his skin caught her off guard. She cleared her throat. "I wanted to thank you for bringing me to the hospital." She looked up and curved her lips into a small smile. "I don't remember exactly what happened, but Sara told me I was unconscious, and you pulled me from my car." His touch was gentle. She shifted in the bed and pulled away her hand.

"It's my job." He smiled. "Anyone traveling behind you would have stopped and done the same."

Aunt Phoebe laughed. "Now, Jackson, don't be so modest. Jackson's a paramedic, but he had the day off today. I think I know him well enough to say he never really goes off duty. Even as a child, he rescued anything he could." She placed her index finger to her chin. "Do you remember Miss Pearson's cat? Marcie… I think it was her name."

Jackson smiled. "Yes, it was."

"Well, she got stuck, and Jackson climbed all the way up a huge oak tree to save her."

A hint of redness covered Jackson's cheeks at her aunt's praise.

"A cat, really? That's commendable of you." Melanie nodded.

A slight smile pulled on one side of his mouth. "It was when I decided what I wanted to do when I grew up."

"Save cats?" Melanie blurted.

Judging by the raised eyebrow Aunt Phoebe threw in her direction, she obviously didn't appreciate the sarcasm.

Jackson pushed his shoulders back. "Well, mostly people, but animals, too, if they need rescuing." He flashed a satisfied smile. "I'll never forget the feeling when I placed Marcie back into Miss Pearson's wrinkled hands. She lived alone for thirty years after her husband died. Marcie was all she had."

"Jackson has always had a good heart." Aunt Phoebe grinned and patted his arm.

Barricaded.

That was what Melanie's heart was now. She would do whatever she had to in order to protect herself from further anguish.

Aunt Phoebe took a seat on the edge of the bed. "You look tired, dear. Maybe we should leave so you can get some rest."

Melanie squirmed, struggling to sit up. "First I need to talk to you about the reason I came to Sweet Gum." She wouldn't let the fact that she'd had an accident and was now in the hospital stop her from telling Aunt Phoebe the truth of her mission.

"You came to get some much-needed rest, child." Aunt Phoebe slipped one arm and then the other into the sleeves of her raincoat.

"Yes, it's true, but the main reason is to bring you back to DC to live with me." She blew out a breath. There, she'd said it.

"What?" Jackson shouted and looked around the room. "Sorry—I didn't mean to raise my voice."

Aunt Phoebe rubbed the top of Melanie's head. "Dear, you're talking crazy. I would never leave Sweet Gum."

Melanie noticed Jackson listening intently. He even shook his head a couple of times.

"Now, you get some rest. Dr. Roberts said you can go home in the morning." Aunt Phoebe leaned over and kissed her cheek. "I'll prepare a big dinner, just like it's Sunday."

She shook her head. "Please, don't go to any trouble for me. Besides, I'm not a big eater."

"Nonsense. You need more meat on your bones." She squeezed Melanie's arm. "I don't know how you keep warm. I'll make you some crispy fried chicken. It's Jackson's favorite." She turned to him. "You save your appetite, too. I'll prepare a meal for the hero…and bring your sweet little girl since school's out again tomorrow for that teacher workday."

Jackson nodded. "Sounds great. Rebecca loves your fried chicken." He looked in Melanie's direction. "Rebecca's my five-year-old daughter."

Aunt Phoebe waved goodbye, and Jackson followed her. The door closed, and they were gone.

The IV drip hummed. Melanie covered her face with a pillow. She wanted to scream. She hadn't come here to mingle with the locals. She just wanted to bring her aunt home. Jackson and his daughter weren't family. Why did her aunt act as though they were related? Melanie took a sip of her water and rolled onto her side.

She wasn't ready to be around children, not yet. Maybe never. She'd tried keeping a journal, like the doctor had suggested, but the pain felt even more real when she'd put her thoughts down on paper. What did her doctor know, anyway? He hadn't lost his children—she'd seen the photo of him and his wife with three smiling boys on the corner of his mahogany desk. She yanked the sheet over her head, wishing she could stay hidden forever, but whether she wanted to or not, tomorrow she'd be having dinner with Jackson and his daughter.

As Jackson headed to the Whitesides' house, his heart pounded. He couldn't wait to see Rebecca. While he drove along their half-mile gravel driveway, his thoughts drifted to Melanie. How dare she suggest moving Phoebe to DC? She'd never even visited and knew nothing about her aunt's life and how happy she was living in the valley. It was obvious Melanie was a woman with a heavy heart, but that didn't give her a right to uproot Phoebe.

He pulled in front of the Whitesides' house and honked the horn. Within seconds, Rebecca flew out the door. He smiled and watched the love of his life, his vivacious daughter, sprint toward his truck. She ran as though she was trying to reach the finish line and he was the prize. For a second, his joy turned to sadness as he wondered how many more years she would think of him as her hero. He pushed the thought away and jumped from the truck with open arms.

"Daddy, can I have a puppy? Please, can I?" Rebecca pleaded and took a giant leap into his arms.

"What? Who wants to sell my baby a puppy?" Jackson decided he'd play around a little with his daughter. He placed her back on the ground.

Rebecca frowned. "I'm not a baby." She put her hands on her hips. "I'll be six in a few months."

"So tell me, what kind of dog is this?" The buzz around town was that Larry Whiteside was breeding a litter of Labrador retrievers.

With eyes wide and as blue as the ocean, Rebecca began to captivate him—as she always did. He'd have been the first to admit he was a softy when it came to his daughter and the things she asked for. "Mr. Whiteside said Sally is going to have her pups soon, and she's big and yellow. He told me I had to ask you first," Rebecca answered.

Jackson scratched his chin. "Let me think about it for a bit. Hmm…well, since our closest neighbors are ten miles down the road and they're seventy-five years old, you just might need a little friend."

Rebecca jumped up and down and then proceeded to twirl. She loved to twirl. "Yes! I'll take care of her. I promise. I've already picked out a name. I want to call her Samantha."

Jackson's heart melted. He could never say no to his little girl. "We have a couple of days before the pups are born, and they will have to stay with their mama for a while." He cupped her chin. "I do have one question for you, sweetie. What happens if all of Sally's puppies are boys? What will you name him?"

"Daddy, come on. I'd call him Sam—duh."

He laughed and gave her a big bear hug. "You've got it all figured out, don't you?"

Larry and Wilma Whiteside, along with their daughter Mary, Rebecca's best friend, stood on their porch as he and his daughter walked to the front door to thank them for having Rebecca over. "Anytime Mary wants to come over for the night, she's always welcome." Jackson smiled as he reached to shake Larry's hand.

As they walked back to the truck, Rebecca looked up. "Can she come tonight since tomorrow's Friday and we don't have school?" He lifted Rebecca in and buckled her seat belt.

"I think you two had enough time together for now. Besides, we have plans tomorrow."

She bounced up and down in her seat. "What are we doing?"

He buckled his seat belt and turned the key in the ignition. "Miss Phoebe has invited us over for an early dinner. Her niece is visiting."

"Is she the lady you rescued?" Rebecca asked and kicked her feet against the back of his seat.

"Where did you hear I rescued someone?"

"I heard Mrs. Whiteside telling Mr. White-side you saved a lady today."

"Yes, she was Miss Phoebe's niece. She's from Washington, DC." He glanced at her in the rearview mirror. "You know where DC is, don't you?"

"Ah...duh, of course—it's our nation's capital." She flashed a lopsided grin in the reflection. Jackson stifled his laugh. He wasn't keen on her using "duh," but sometimes it was too darn cute.

"Is she pretty?" The kicking subsided. "What's her name?"

His grip tightened on the steering wheel. "Her name is Miss Melanie." Her face flashed in his mind, and his pulse quickened. "Yes, she's very pretty." He swallowed hard. *Too pretty.* What had he been thinking when he agreed to dinner?

Chapter Two

"Jackson and Rebecca won't be here for a couple of hours," Aunt Phoebe announced from her kitchen. "Why don't you go lie down and take a little nap?"

Melanie squeezed her eyes tightly shut. The searing pain persisted in her neck. She'd been anxious to leave the hospital this morning, but now she wondered if she should have stayed. With the tips of her fingers, she touched the stitches on her cheek. No point trying to cover them with makeup. She stared out the living-room window in dreaded anticipation of the dinner guests, especially Jackson's daughter.

Aunt Phoebe's house, a charming country cottage, reminded Melanie of the gingerbread houses she'd made with her mother as a child. Although small in comparison to her three-level town house in the heart of Capitol Hill, Aunt

Phoebe's cottage sat on fifteen acres of immaculate tree-lined property, obviously maintained by a professional landscaper. Melanie had to admit it was stunning. The backyard exploded with shades of yellow and red. A quaint white gazebo sat near a small pond. Potted mums perfectly arranged along the interior of the structure provided an added pop of dazzling autumn colors.

Once upon a time, this had been her favorite time of the year, but no more. Her world was the same no matter the season. *Dark.*

Melanie peeled herself from the comfort of the La-Z-Boy chair. Now was a good time to discuss the move. Before Jackson showed up. She'd sensed his displeasure at the suggestion when she'd brought it up yesterday. She pushed through the swinging door that led to the kitchen. The combination of the bright October sun and the yellow-painted walls made her feel like she needed her sunglasses. "Aunt Phoebe, don't you think it might be time for you to slow down? Have someone look after you for a change? You're sixty-five years old. You can't expect to continue to take care of this house and run The Bean." As far as Melanie knew, she worked there every weekday and Saturday. And Melanie suspected the only reason she didn't work on Sunday was because they were closed.

Aunt Phoebe was a firm believer in going to church on Sunday and spending the rest of the day in fellowship with family and neighbors.

"Slow down?" Phoebe speared a piece of chicken with a fork and placed it on a floured baking sheet. "I'm hitting my stride." She pushed out her chest. "In fact, I just signed up for the hospital's 5K."

Melanie's mouth dropped open. "You can't run. You'll injure yourself."

"Maybe I can't run, but I can certainly walk. It's for children's cancer research, and if I have to, I'll crawl across the finish line." She sprinkled some pepper onto the chicken and rolled it in the flour. She turned her head when the pepper triggered a sneeze. "Excuse me."

Nothing slowed the woman down. But in spite of how she felt now, if something happened to her, Melanie would find herself alone in the world. Her stomach turned at the thought. "So, what do you think about moving to DC with me?" She stared down at the chicken.

Aunt Phoebe shook her head. "Honestly, when you mentioned this crazy idea at the hospital, I thought you were joking. Why would I want to move? My life is here."

The oven beeped. It was fully preheated and ready for the oversize biscuits.

Melanie expelled a weary sigh. "You're the only family I have. I want to take care of you."

Aunt Phoebe snatched the checkered dish towel off of the counter and dried her hands. "You don't think I'm capable of looking out for myself?"

"I'm sorry. I didn't mean to offend you. I just think your home and The Coffee Bean are a lot of upkeep for anyone."

"You mean for an old coot like me?" She tightened the strings on her apron. "This is nonsense. The valley is where I plan to spend my last days on this earth, however long the good Lord determines I have." She patted Melanie's arm. "Let's end this subject. We've got company coming."

"Don't you get scared living out here alone?"

"Scared? Why would I be scared?" She pulled on her yellow gloves and, with an oversize sponge, scrubbed the cast-iron skillet with the tenacity of a twenty-year-old. "Besides, God is always watching over me. I trust Him to take care of me."

Melanie dropped her arms to her sides. Her aunt was stubborn.

"What about you?" Aunt Phoebe set the skillet in the sink, took off the gloves and reached for Melanie's hand. She guided her to the kitchen table, and they each took a seat across from one another. "Not a day goes by I don't think about you living alone in that big ol' town house. The loss you've suffered is more than anyone should ever endure in a lifetime." Aunt Phoebe reached over the bowl of Golden Delicious apples to wipe the tear that escaped Melanie's eye. Her touch was warm. "God has a plan for you. He'll carry you through this, but you must have faith. And in the end, you'll find peace."

Melanie yanked her hand from Aunt Phoebe's grasp. She stood and paced the kitchen floor. "Why would God steal my family? They were my world, Aunt Phoebe." She turned toward the kitchen window. A chipmunk hopped along the split-rail fence. "Where was He when my children were trapped inside a burning car, while their father did everything in his power to save them but died trying?"

"Oh child, God will bring you through this difficulty if you'll open your heart to Him."

Melanie shook her head. "I'm not sure I can believe in Him again. I did once. I really did... but not anymore." She turned from the window and walked toward the table. Her throat parched, she reached for her glass of water and took three large gulps before placing it back on the table. "I didn't come here to upset you— please believe me. It's just—" she picked up the glass and drained it "—I can't seem to get my life back on track. I don't know how to live without my family." Chill bumps peppered her skin as her aunt took her hand.

"Put your trust in God, and in time, peace will flourish."

Melanie gave Aunt Phoebe's hand a quick squeeze. "If you don't mind, I think I'll go lie down for a little while—" her footsteps tapped across the hardwood floors before she turned back around and faced her aunt "—unless you need my help."

"No, of course not. I've got everything under control." She walked toward the sink.

Inside the guest room, Melanie gazed up at the cedar ceiling. Her hand gripped the cold doorknob as she slowly pushed the door shut.

Peace. She hadn't felt it since the last time she kissed her girls and husband goodbye.

A cold chill ran through her blood when, across the room, she spied the gift she'd mailed to Aunt Phoebe on her last birthday. Sluggishly she walked toward the dresser and picked up the present.

She studied the photo inside the frame, and her eyes erupted with tears. It was from the last trip they'd taken to the beach as a family. Her husband, Jeff, had asked a stranger passing by to take their picture. Tan and smiling, they had an amazing life. Her hands trembled as she placed the frame on the dresser. She wanted to crawl inside the photo and be with her family one more time. Her body quivered, and instead she crawled into the bed and sobbed.

After what felt like hours, but had probably just been one, Melanie entered the kitchen to the sound of chicken sizzling in the skillet. "I'm sorry, Aunt Phoebe. I should be helping you."

Her aunt flung the dish towel over her shoulder and brushed her hand across her forehead, leaving behind a trail of flour. "You need your rest." She patted Melanie's arm. "Besides, I've been cooking like this for over forty years. Making dinner for four is easy peasy."

Melanie yanked a paper towel from the roll, turned on the faucet and swiped the towel under the water. "Here, let me at least do this." She smiled. "You've got a little flour on your forehead," she said, wiping away the powdery substance. She took in her aunt's features. Despite a few wrinkles and hair as white as snow, her aunt still looked youthful.

"Thanks, dear. Oh, I think I hear a car."

Melanie's pulse rose. She listened to the sound of tires crunching on the gravel driveway. "I'll go get the door," she told her aunt. A chill traveled through her body as she walked toward the entrance. She wrapped her arms around herself. This wouldn't be easy, but her aunt seemed happy, so she pasted a smile on her face and flung open the door. A flash of blond hair tore past Melanie.

The sound of prancing feet scurrying along the hardwood floor filled the room. "Phoebe, Phoebe…we're here!"

She tried to catch her breath, her legs weak. She couldn't do this. She wasn't ready to be around children. Not yet. The child's blond ringlets sprouting from her head bounced like rubber balls when she turned and headed back toward the door. Melanie glanced down when the girl stopped in front of her. She wore a yellow dress covered in red polka dots. Her shoes were patent leather, and exactly like the ones Melanie had purchased over a year ago. Her stomach wrenched.

"Hello, I'm pleased to meet you. I'm Rebecca." The child looked up, extended her tiny hand and grinned. The smile lit up her entire face. Wide-eyed, she turned toward the door. "And that's my daddy." She giggled. "Oh yeah, you already know him. Remember, he's the one who rescued you yesterday. He's right. You're pretty." She released her hand and raced toward Aunt Phoebe as she exited the kitchen.

Melanie's stomach churned. Did he really think she was pretty? She might have misunderstood. He was probably talking about the nurse. What was her name again? Yes, Sara. She appeared to have a crush on Jackson. They were probably dating. Not that Melanie cared either way. She didn't want anyone to think she was pretty. She didn't want people to think anything of her—she wished she were invisible. It would have been much easier.

"Hello, Rebecca. You look lovely today." Aunt Phoebe took the child into her arms and gave her a kiss on her cheek.

Rebecca pulled back, her arms still around Aunt Phoebe's neck. Their noses nearly touched. "Guess what? I'm getting a puppy."

In a daze, Melanie watched Rebecca. It seemed like an eternity since she'd felt a child's arms around her neck. Would she ever feel the softness of children's smooth and flawless skin? Would she ever smell the sweetness when they were fresh out of the bathtub? She jumped when a hand touched her shoulder, erasing her negative thoughts, at least for now.

She turned and found herself face-to-face with Jackson.

A slow smile moved across his mouth. "I'm sorry. I didn't mean to scare you." He held two bunches of pink roses. "These are for you." He handed her one bunch. How did he know they were her favorite? Her father had given her pink roses when she'd graduated from law school.

It was the last gift she'd received from him. A single rose, now brown and crinkled, remained in her memory book, along with photographs from her life before it'd ended.

"You didn't scare me." She accepted the roses and swiped the bouquet under her nose. It seemed forever since she'd smelled the sweet scent of fresh-cut roses. "They're beautiful." She took another sniff. "It was thoughtful of you to bring them. Thank you."

His focus remained on her. "Your color is better today. How are you feeling?"

His scrutiny made her face burn, but somehow, in the last couple of minutes, she'd forgotten about the pain in her neck and the rest of her body aches. "I'm feeling okay. Thanks for asking." She played with a strand of her hair.

"Hello, Jackson. What do you have there?" Aunt Phoebe wiped her hands down her Kiss the Chef apron.

He smiled and handed the other bouquet to Aunt Phoebe. "These are for you, a thank-you for having me and Rebecca over."

"Dear, put these in some water. We'll use them as the centerpiece." She handed Melanie the roses. Melanie headed toward the kitchen, inhaling the fragrance once more. The clicking of tiny feet came from behind and she turned.

"I know where the vases are, Miss Melanie. Can I help?"

Startled by Rebecca's enthusiasm, Melanie nodded. Without warning, Rebecca grabbed hold of her free hand and led her into the kitchen. Melanie's heart melted. She wanted to cry, but instead, she forced a smile, allowing the hand to remain as they entered the kitchen.

Melanie watched Rebecca take command. She certainly knew her way around Aunt Phoebe's kitchen, finding the exact cupboard where vases of all sizes and colors were stored.

"Do you like this one, Miss Melanie?" She turned holding a white vase with tiny yellow daisies covering the sides, and large enough for both bouquets. "I love daisies, don't you?"

"Yes, I do." Melanie straightened her shoulders. She could do this. All she had to do was make it through a couple of hours. Surely they wouldn't stay longer than two hours. "I think it's a perfect choice."

Melanie filled the vase with water and carefully arranged the roses. "How do they look?"

Rebecca nodded and smiled. "They look beautiful. You're really nice, Miss Melanie. Do you have any kids my age?"

The yellow walls began to close in around her, and the kitchen whirled. Melanie tried to make it to the table, but her legs were weak. She had to sit. Without warning, the vase slipped from her hands and crashed to the floor.

The sounds of muffled voices filled the room.

"Melanie! Are you okay?" Aunt Phoebe raced to her side. "Did you cut yourself?"

"No, I'm fine."

Aunt Phoebe placed her hand across Melanie's arm. "Do you feel dizzy? Maybe you should go lie down? I'll keep the chicken warm in the oven."

"No, please, I'm okay. Let me clean up this mess so we can eat," Melanie announced and pushed her hair from her eyes.

Jackson stepped forward. "Rebecca and I will clean this up. Phoebe, take Melanie into the family room."

"Daddy, is Miss Melanie okay? I just asked her if she had any kids my age, and she dropped the vase."

Melanie glanced toward Jackson. Their eyes connected before she looked away. "I'm fine, Rebecca. The vase was wet. It just slipped. No big deal." She turned and headed into the family room with her aunt.

"You should sit down for a while?" Phoebe guided her toward the leather sofa. "We'll take care of things in the kitchen."

Melanie wondered what Jackson and Rebecca must think of her. How could she enjoy a meal with them when she couldn't even fill a vase with water? "I'm okay. I want to help."

Her aunt just smiled. "Rest for a bit. I'll call you when dinner's on the table." She turned and walked back to the kitchen.

Melanie flopped down on the sofa. She knew she wasn't truly fine. Her reaction to Rebecca's mention of children was proof she was still hurting inside. This past year, she'd lived in a murky world, simply going through the motions of each day. She didn't care about anything or anyone. Her dramatic weight loss was proof that she didn't care about herself, either. Heaviness staked out a permanent residence inside her chest. A lump formed in her throat, and the tears escaped down her cheeks. If she could have gone back in time, she would have been the one driving the car instead of her exhausted husband…but she couldn't go back. Her family was gone, and she'd carry the guilt with her for the rest of her life.

An hour later, Jackson leaned back in his chair. He placed his hand on his stomach and rubbed in a circular motion. "Every time you make fried chicken, Phoebe, it's crispier than the last batch." He picked up his napkin and placed it to his lips. A quick look at Melanie's plate proved what she'd said yesterday. She wasn't a big eater. "Are you sure you're feeling okay, Melanie? You've hardly touched your meal."

She fingered her necklace. "I don't have much of an appetite. Maybe it's from the pain medication I've been taking."

Phoebe picked up the bowl of mashed potatoes and scooped a heaping spoonful. "These always taste good to me when I have an upset stomach."

Melanie nodded and held out her plate. Jackson watched while she picked at her food like a child. Finally she tried the mashed potatoes. "These are delicious."

"So, Phoebe tells me you're a divorce attorney. Sounds like interesting work." Jackson snatched a pinch of corn bread and popped it into his mouth. "I'm sure it's never dull."

"My mommy and daddy got divorced," Rebecca announced. "I don't remember her. She left when I was really little." She quickly looked down. "I'm sorry."

Jackson observed Melanie place her hand on top of Rebecca's hand. "It's okay. You can talk about your mommy if you want to."

He nodded when Rebecca looked at him for confirmation. "She had really dark hair, kind of like yours, but shorter. I have a picture of her on my nightstand. You can come see it sometime if you want to." She smiled. "Daddy said she liked to dance, and she was a good singer, too." She tucked a stray curl that had escaped from her ponytail behind her ear. "I think she left us to become famous." Staring out the window, she placed her fist underneath her chin and tilted her head. "I think she'll come back for me…for both of us, someday."

Jackson's heart ached for his daughter. The anger toward his ex-wife boiled to the surface every so often. Would the scars ever heal? Rebecca missed her, but it was a blessing she was too young to have witnessed her mother's behavior. He'd rather she have good thoughts of her than remember the way things really were.

"Okay, who's ready for a big hunk of Phoebe's chocolate sour cream layer cake?" He looked at Melanie, and then Phoebe, and saw that both were wiping away tears.

Thankfully Rebecca hadn't noticed how emotional the ladies had become. She sprang from her chair at the mention of the dessert. "I'll get the plates and forks," she yelled and ran toward the kitchen.

Phoebe cleared her throat. "I think I'll go help." She turned and shot a wink at Melanie. "I only allow one disaster a day in my kitchen."

When her aunt left the room, Melanie turned to Jackson. "I wouldn't call a broken vase a disaster."

"She was only joking," he said. "What happened in the kitchen earlier could have happened to anyone." He sipped his iced tea. "I'm sorry if Rebecca upset you."

The silence was deafening. Melanie played with the condensation on her glass. He studied her face and wished he could take away the sadness.

She raised her head and looked him in the eye. "Your daughter is so sweet. Nothing she says could upset me. I guess I'm still rattled from the accident."

Obviously she wasn't going to share what really bothered her. He understood. They'd just met, and opening up to someone required trust, something he'd definitely lacked the past several years. "Jackson, I'm sorry about your wife. I'm sure it's been difficult on you and Rebecca."

He shrugged his shoulders, not ready to share, either. Yes, she was Phoebe's niece, but he knew nothing about her. Less than twenty-four hours ago, their lives were separate from each other. Now, after an accident, their worlds had merged. But could he ever trust a woman who obviously didn't put family first? She never visited her aunt though she lived only a couple of hours away. He wasn't ready to confide in her, or any woman, for that matter.

"Rebecca and I get along fine." He drained

the last of his iced tea and reached for the pitcher. "Would you like some more?"

She shook her head.

Jackson filled his glass. "So, what prompted you finally to make a trip to see Phoebe? From what I understand, she's been trying to get you to the valley for years. Too busy with your hot-shot career, I suppose?"

She lifted her chin, and a moment passed before she spoke. "Like I mentioned yesterday at the hospital, I've come to convince Aunt Phoebe to move back to DC with me." She held her shoulders straight, like a soldier in formation. "She's getting older. It's time she had family nearby."

Jackson's spine stiffened. "I didn't think you were serious. Phoebe's life is here." His heart raced at the thought of Phoebe moving.

Melanie tapped her finger against her empty glass. "I'm her only family, Jackson. She belongs with me." Her eyes kept a strong hold on his. "You asked what brought me here, and I told you. Can we please drop this conversation? I don't want her to hear us. She needs time to adjust to the idea."

"She won't adjust," he snapped. "Besides, she has family here—Rebecca and me."

"You're not blood, Jackson."

"You don't need the same blood in order to

be family. If you cared about her, you wouldn't take her away from the only life she knows and loves." He bolted from the chair. It screeched along the hardwood floor.

"What in the world is going on out here?" Phoebe stood in the doorway with both hands on her hips.

"Melanie was just telling me a little more about your move." He eyed Melanie, waiting for her to pounce.

Phoebe laughed. "We've discussed it already. I'm not moving and that's final."

"You haven't had enough time to make a final decision." Melanie walked toward her aunt and reached out for her hand.

Ignoring the extended hand, Phoebe paced the dining-room floor. "I don't need more time." She picked up her glass of water and took two long swigs. "What on earth has put such a crazy idea into your head? It needs to stop—now."

Jackson took notice of Phoebe's complexion. She looked pale, and tiny beads of perspiration dotted her forehead. "Are you okay, Phoebe?"

She yanked a tissue from her apron pocket and blotted her forehead. "It's just a little warm in here from the oven. I'm fine." She slipped the tissue back into her pocket. "So, what do you think about Melanie's plan, Jackson?"

He shook his head. "I think it's a bad one. Your life is here with the people who love you."

"I agree. And I won't discuss this any further," Phoebe announced.

"Wait, please," Melanie said. "I'm not trying to ruin your life. I love you, and I don't want you to be alone."

"I'm staying put...end of discussion." Phoebe turned and headed back to the kitchen.

Jackson ran his hand down the front of his face, relieved the conversation was over, at least for now.

Melanie, on the other hand, did not look pleased.

"Daddy, come quick!" Rebecca's scream had him sprinting toward the kitchen like a jackrabbit.

He burst through the door and saw Phoebe lying on the floor.

Melanie entered the kitchen and gasped. "Jackson, help her." She raced to her aunt's side. "What's happening?"

Jackson heard Phoebe's garbled speech and noticed the side of her mouth was drooping. "She's having a stroke. I've got to get her to the hospital. Now!"

Melanie gripped his wrist. "Shouldn't we call for the ambulance?"

He shook his head. "No, we can't wait." He

scooped Phoebe's tiny frame into his arms and headed toward the door. "You take Rebecca in your car. Don't try to keep up. I'll meet you at the hospital."

"Daddy… I'm scared."

Jackson stopped at the front door and turned. "Everything will be okay. You go with Miss Melanie."

Chapter Three

Melanie grabbed Rebecca's hand and raced through the ER entrance. She'd never imagined she'd be at this hospital—or holding a child's hand—again. *Doesn't Jackson know how difficult this is—being around a child?* Of course not. She hadn't allowed Aunt Phoebe to share her past with anyone.

"Rebecca, over here." Jackson jumped from a brown sofa and scooped his daughter into his arms.

"How's Aunt Phoebe?" Melanie's pulse raced. "Has the doctor come out yet?"

"No, not yet." He placed Rebecca on the ground. "You'll need to check in with Sara at the desk. She needs some information from you. I'm going to take Rebecca down to the playroom."

Before Melanie knew what was happening,

Rebecca had her arms tight around her waist. Her breath froze in her chest. She needed to break free.

"Daddy, I want to stay here with Miss Melanie."

There was something about this little girl, but she had to play it safe—keep her distance. "You go with your daddy. I have to fill out some paperwork so the doctor can take care of Aunt Phoebe."

The smell of coffee wafted from behind the front desk as she walked over.

"Hi, Melanie. Do you remember me?"

"Of course. How are you, Sara?"

The nurse organized some forms and attached them to a clipboard. "I'm doing well. I'm sorry about Phoebe." She handed Melanie the documents. "Dr. Roberts is here. He got called in on another emergency, but he'll be caring for her."

Melanie took the papers and forced a smile.

"Just complete what you can. We already have her insurance information in our system."

When Jackson returned and approached the desk, Melanie watched Sara's face light up like a beacon.

"Hello there, Jackson," Sara said. She fluffed the back of her hair and batted her false eyelashes.

Melanie stared at Jackson. A pang of jealousy

took hold. Why would she be jealous over a man she hardly knew? Sure, he was gorgeous, and he seemed like a good father, but jealous—no way. Besides, he was nothing but a roadblock to her plan. Still, when he appeared oblivious to Sara's flirtation, she felt relieved.

"Hey, Sara. Can you let Dr. Roberts know we're here? We'll be in the waiting area until he's ready to speak with Melanie."

Sara's smile faded, and she jutted her chin out. "Sure, Jackson." She turned on her heel and strutted down the hall.

Jackson pointed at four chairs lined close together in front of a floor-to-ceiling window. "Let's have a seat over here. Do you want something to drink?"

"No, thank you." Melanie sat in one of the brown vinyl chairs and gazed out the window. A brisk wind whipped through the courtyard. Leaves fell from the trees and swirled along the ground. She noticed a man walking with two little girls, probably his children. Where was the mother? She was probably at work. Melanie's heart sank.

Jackson blew a heavy breath and leaned back into his chair. "Look, Melanie, you were right. I should have stopped discussing the move when you asked. If I had, maybe Phoebe wouldn't be here."

She rubbed her hands across her arms. Why were hospitals so cold? There were those annoying fluorescent lights buzzing. "No, the move was my idea." Melanie leaned forward and put her hands over her face.

After a few moments of sobbing, she peeled her hands away and shot Jackson a look. She closed her eyes, shaken by the truth. "I'm the reason she had the stroke, Jackson." Tears gushed for the present and for the past. "I should have never come here."

A shiver ran down her spine when he placed a hand on the small of her back.

"You're talking crazy, Mel."

Another shiver.

It was the first time he'd called her Mel. She liked it. Why did it sound good coming from his lips? Melanie pushed aside the thought.

Jackson moved his hand in tiny circular motions along her back. "Phoebe's stroke didn't happen because you want to move her to DC." He paused, reached for a tissue from the table next to his chair and turned her face toward his. Her breath caught in her throat for a moment when she saw the tenderness in his eyes. With a gentle touch, he wiped the tears from her face.

Though she knew he meant only to offer comfort, his kind gesture made her edgy. Melanie took the tissue from Jackson and looked away.

Over the next hour, Melanie paced the floor, waiting for Dr. Roberts to give her an update on Aunt Phoebe. Periodically she glanced at Jackson, who spent much of his time in prayer. At least, that was what she thought he was doing. His head was down and his eyes were closed. His lips moved ever so slightly. Did he really think that God listened? If that were the case, she'd still have a family.

As though Jackson heard her thoughts, he looked up. "Do you want to pray for Phoebe together?"

She shook her head and turned away. With her arms crossed, she gazed out the window once more. The man and children she'd seen earlier were gone. A pain filled her gut. Gone... like her family.

Jackson stood and came toward where she was standing. "Do you not believe?"

"Believe what?" Her eyebrow arched.

"That the power of prayer is unstoppable. Nothing is ever wasted when you share it with Him, Mel." He reached for her hand. "Whatever it is you're dealing with, He's there for you."

His hand was warm. She found comfort in his touch. Afraid of what might happen if it remained, she jerked from his grip. "I'm sorry, Jackson, but I don't believe that."

Silence permeated the air. Several minutes

later, Sara entered the room. "Excuse me. Dr. Roberts will be out to speak with you within the half hour. We're busy today."

"Thank you, Sara." Melanie took a seat and released a heavy sigh. She prepared herself for the worst. After the past year, what else could she expect?

Jackson sat down and turned toward Melanie. "Phoebe is a strong woman of faith." He bit down on his lip. "And she's pretty stubborn, too."

She smiled and nodded in agreement. Would she continue to be stubborn about the move? Melanie turned her attention back to the window, hoping to see the family once more.

Forty-five minutes later, Jackson spotted Dr. Roberts. He saw the man stop at the nurses' station and hand some papers to the nurse working with Sara. He continued down the hall.

"Hello. I'm sorry you had to wait so long. The ER's bustling this afternoon." He paused and glanced at Melanie. "Have you been feeling alright since the accident? You look a little pale."

"Yes, I'm fine. How's Aunt Phoebe?"

Dr. Roberts referred to his clipboard and looked up. "The tests confirmed it was a stroke. Thankfully you got her here when you did. Any later and it could have been much worse."

Jackson watched Melanie. She shook her head. Her shoulders stiffened. "This is my fault, Dr. Roberts," she said.

The doctor scratched his temple and looked at Jackson before turning back to Melanie. "What in the world would make you say such a thing? You certainly didn't cause her stroke."

She threw a look toward Jackson. "She's upset because I want to move her to DC."

Dr. Roberts's eyebrow arched. "Move to DC? Phoebe?"

"Dr. Roberts." Jackson shook his head. He hoped the doctor would understand now wasn't the time to discuss an impending move. "You were saying about Phoebe's condition?"

The doctor pulled a seat in front of the couple and removed his glasses. He rubbed his eyes for a moment. "She's having some trouble with her speech, and there's definitely partial paralysis on her left side."

"Paralysis!" Melanie sprang from her chair and walked toward the window. With her arms wrapped around her waist, she turned and looked at Dr. Roberts with wide eyes. "Will it be permanent?"

Placing his glasses on, he flipped through his papers. Dr. Roberts motioned for Jackson to bring Melanie back to her chair.

His boots pecked on the tile like a redheaded

woodpecker as he walked over to her. Melanie flinched when he rested his hand on her arm. "Please, have a seat."

She shadowed Jackson and sat down. Her breaths were short and rapid while she fidgeted in her chair. "I'm sorry, but she's all the family I have, Dr. Roberts."

Jackson's heart ached for Melanie. Even though she never visited, it was obvious she loved her aunt. He reached over and held her hand. "She'll be okay, Melanie."

"Will Aunt Phoebe need rehabilitation?"

"Yes, she'll need speech and physical therapy to strengthen her muscles." The sound of the doctor scribbling notes filled the room while they both absorbed the news.

Dr. Roberts looked up and laid his pen on the clipboard. "Madison Village is an excellent facility in Harrisonburg. I've already called to check room availability."

"How long will she have to stay?" Melanie twisted a tissue between her fingers.

"The paralysis won't be permanent, but I can't say how much time it will take to go away. Phoebe is incredibly strong, so ideally she'll be back to normal soon. You'll have to take care of The Bean, Jackson."

A knot squeezed in Jackson's stomach. With everything happening, he hadn't thought about that. "Of course. I'll make sure it's running smoothly."

Melanie's eyes narrowed. "Wait a minute, Jackson. It's Phoebe's business, too, and she's *my* aunt. I'll take care of the restaurant. Unless you don't think I can handle it. I do have a law degree, you know."

Dr. Roberts's laughter filled the room. "Okay, you two, there's enough to do at The Bean for everyone." He smiled. "Why don't you work together? Phoebe would appreciate it."

"What about your job, Jackson?" Her lips pursed.

Yesterday had been his first day off in a very long time, and he was on the schedule to return to duty tomorrow. He rarely took a vacation, so he had a lot of leave accumulated. Four years ago, he and Taylor had taken Rebecca on her first trip to the Outer Banks of North Carolina. Rebecca was just learning to walk. He smiled as he recalled the framed photograph on his bedroom dresser. It was a photo of her first footprints in the sand. That was the last time they were together as a family. His world had never been the same.

"Yes, I do go back tomorrow, but I'll talk to Tom tonight. I've got the time, so it won't be a problem."

Melanie rubbed her brow. "I really don't think it's necessary."

"The Bean is just as important to me as it is to Phoebe. I'm half owner. If anyone is going to run the place while she's recovering, it's me." Jackson's jaw clenched. Why did this woman have to make everything so difficult? "Plus, won't your big city law firm need you?"

Dr. Roberts shot Jackson a questioning look. He stood when the intercom announced he was needed in the ER. "Well, it's agreed, then. You'll *both* help Phoebe."

Melanie nodded and glanced at Jackson. He returned a nod and shook the doctor's hand. "When do you plan to move Phoebe to the rehab facility?" Melanie asked.

"I'll call on Monday morning and schedule her for admission on Tuesday. Of course, that's subject to change if there are any complications."

Melanie's eyes popped. "Complications, like what? I thought you said she'd be okay."

"Don't worry. Let's take this one day at a time."

Melanie wrapped her index finger around her purse strap. "Thank you for everything, Dr. Roberts. Aunt Phoebe spoke very highly of you after my accident." She stood, placed her purse on her chair and gave the doctor a hug.

She didn't let go until the intercom paged him again.

"I have to go. You two should head home and get some rest. It's been an emotional afternoon." He started to walk away, but stopped and turned around. "And, Melanie, you should give up the idea of moving Phoebe."

"I agree," Jackson said as he glanced at his watch. He needed to get Rebecca home and settled in for the night.

Melanie didn't acknowledge either of their comments. She appeared lost in thought.

Jackson cleared his throat. "Dr. Roberts, before we leave, could Melanie visit with Phoebe for a moment?"

Melanie's eyes brightened. "Oh yes, can I see her?"

"I don't see why not. I'll send Sara. She'll take you."

"Thanks again, Doc." Jackson shook his hand and thought about what a blessing this man was to their community. Once Phoebe returned to her old self again, he planned to do a little matchmaking.

"What are you grinning about?" Melanie asked as she crossed her arms over her chest.

"Oh, nothing." He tried to erase the grin.

She rolled her eyes and sat down. "Look, Jackson, about The Bean. Why don't we cover it in shifts? Since it's only open from 7:00 a.m. until 2:00 p.m. for breakfast and lunch, I can take the first three-and-a-half hours and you the second, or vice versa." She tucked a loose strand of hair behind her ear. "Or we could alternate days. There's no need for us both to be there at the same time."

Jackson laughed and shook his head. "You don't think there's a need for both of us to cover it?" He rubbed his chin. "There's no way you could handle the crowd alone, especially on a Saturday...with or without a law degree."

Her knee bounced in agitation. "I think I'm perfectly capable of handling a little country restaurant."

She didn't have a clue. "Phoebe has a $4.99 breakfast special on Saturday. It comes with two eggs, two pancakes and two slices of bacon or sausage links, and to drink, orange juice and coffee. It draws a crowd." Jackson's stomach growled.

She arched her brow. "I hope there's a gym in the area. It doesn't sound healthy. How do people do anything else after such a big meal?"

He slid her a sideways stare. "Most folks around here have a working farm, and believe me, they get their workout."

"I doubt they get their heart rate up riding around on a tractor."

Jackson clenched his teeth. "We might not have a fancy gym like you're used to, but trust me, we get our heart rates up every day." He hesitated. "In fact, right now mine is through the roof."

"I didn't mean to offend you. I just think The Bean should offer a healthier menu."

Sara approached the couple. "Melanie, if you want to see Phoebe, you can follow me to her room."

Melanie looked at Jackson. "Do you want to go?"

"No, you go, but give her a kiss for me."

While Melanie visited with Phoebe, Jackson spent the time alone in prayer.

Ten minutes later, she returned with a huge smile splashed on her face. "Aunt Phoebe looked good, better than I thought she would. She couldn't speak clearly, but I'm sure it will improve in time."

Relieved to see Melanie more at ease, he glanced at his watch. "Let's go get Rebecca, and I'll walk you to your car." He slipped on his leather jacket. "Before we go, let's get back to the schedule at The Bean."

Melanie spoke without hesitation. "I think you're right. We both need to work together, for Aunt Phoebe."

Jackson scratched the top of his head. Melanie had surprised him. She'd been so adamant about working alone. Why the sudden change? Was this all part of her scheme to move Phoebe?

"I don't get it."

"Get what?"

"Just a while ago, you didn't want me near The Bean while you're there. And now—"

Her eyes softened, twisting his stomach inside out. "Aunt Phoebe told me you're like a son to her, and that you know The Bean better than anyone. I know how important it is to her, so I promised when I went back to see her that we'd work side by side."

Jackson gestured in the direction of the front doors. "Okay, then. Let's go."

That evening, Jackson settled into his favorite leather chair in the corner of his bedroom. Thoughts of Melanie swirled in his head. Through the open plantation shutters, the hunter's moon gleamed across the backyard. A coyote he'd seen hanging around for the past week stopped in his tracks and took a peek toward the window before scurrying into the woods.

He turned his attention from that view and ran his hand along the soft, worn leather arms. For thirty years, this chair had sat in his father's insurance office. He missed his dad.

With heavy thoughts about Melanie and her

plan to move Phoebe, he reached for the worn Bible given to him by his paternal grandmother. It had once belonged to his grandfather.

Jackson opened the Bible to his favorite verse. *Trust in the Lord with all your heart and lean not to your own understanding.* After his ex-wife, Taylor, left him and Rebecca for his best friend, Wilson, he meditated on these words daily. He did trust the Lord. It was other people, especially women, where he struggled.

"Daddy, I'm ready for my story."

He closed the Bible. His heart melted at the sight of his daughter standing in the doorway. Dressed in her favorite Winnie the Pooh footed pajamas, she brushed a wild blond curl away from her eyes and sprinted across the room. Gigi, her favorite blanket, trailed behind her along the hardwood floor.

With one soaring leap, she was in his lap. He nuzzled his nose into her hair and smiled. She smelled of sweet honeysuckle from her bubble bath earlier in the evening. Their cuddle time always comforted him. He cherished this time with his daughter. The teenage years would be here in a flash, so he planned to savor every moment.

He kissed the top of her head. "Are you excited for the fair tomorrow?"

She rubbed her sleepy eyes. "Uh-huh. Mr.

Whiteside said he'll take me and Mary on the Ferris wheel. I hope I don't get scared."

When she'd been three, for some unknown reason, Rebecca had developed a slight fear of heights. "I think you'll be just fine. Did you pick out the book you want to read to me tonight?"

She brushed Gigi along her pink cheek. "No, I'll let you pick tonight." Rebecca stared up at him through wide, innocent eyes. "Daddy, why is Miss Melanie so sad?"

It amazed Jackson how intuitive she was. When he was her age, his world had revolved around toys, not paying attention to people's emotions. He ran his hand through her silky curls. "What makes you think she's sad, sweetheart?"

She picked at a loose thread hanging from Gigi. "She has sad eyes."

Jackson wasn't sure what to say. He thought the same thing. After Melanie dropped the vase in the kitchen, she'd been distant during dinner. He could only guess it had to do with Rebecca's question about children. "She's probably just tired. Remember, she had a rough day yesterday traveling, and then the accident. She just needs a good dose of crisp mountain air."

He was happy when she looked up and seemed content with his answer. In truth, he believed there was a lot more to Melanie's sad eyes.

Chapter Four

"I couldn't sleep last night, so I came in early," Melanie said to Jackson as he walked into The Bean. She ran her fingers across her brow.

By the look on Jackson's face, he was surprised to see her behind the counter. "I hope you don't mind." She continued wrapping the silverware with cloth napkins.

Jackson sauntered toward her, wearing a mischievous smile and perfect-fitting blue jeans. He was tall and solid muscle—and looked better than she remembered.

"I didn't think you city people woke up so early." He took a seat, planted his right elbow on the counter and rested his palm under his chin.

Why did her aunt's business partner have to look like he just stepped off a magazine cover? Heat filled her face. "Well, I thought you country folk woke up with the chickens."

"Boy, you must be doing a lot of cooking in the kitchen. You look flushed." He rubbed his unshaven chin.

His handsome good looks were rapidly being overshadowed by his annoying behavior. She took a deep breath and released it. "Are you just going to sit there and watch me, or are you going to help me get the silverware ready?"

He stood. Melanie eyed him while he strutted behind the counter and grabbed two coffeepots. "Restaurant 101—have this ready and make sure it's piping hot." He scooped the grounds into the filter and poured the water into the top of the machine. "People around here expect their caffeine fix as soon as they arrive. They don't have time to wait around."

With his arrogant attitude, he was getting on her last nerve. She rolled her eyes. "Yeah, I guess they have to get busy shoveling horse manure and feeding the chickens."

His laughter filled the restaurant. "I suppose you think we're a bunch of country bumpkins." Then he raised his chin, and his smile faded. "You don't know a thing about the people who live here. Unlike in your big city, we know our neighbors, and we help each other."

When the bell on the door chimed, it prevented her from telling him he didn't know a thing about her city, either. Melanie came from behind the counter and approached the elderly man dressed in bib overalls and a cap. He reminded her of a train engineer. "Good morning. Please, take a seat anywhere."

Both men laughed.

What was so funny?

"Hey, Harry. How are you this morning?" Jackson poured a cup of coffee and placed it at the end of the counter. Wearing a smirk, he threw a glance in Melanie's direction. "Harry's been coming to The Bean every morning for the past twenty years. He owns this end of the counter."

Harry approached and took his seat. He sipped his hot beverage and placed the cup back on the counter. "This is good, Jackson. You make it nice and strong, just the way I like it." He took another sip and looked toward Melanie and back at Jackson. "Who's she?"

Feeling like a complete outsider, Melanie walked toward Harry and extended her hand. "I'm Melanie Harper. Phoebe is my aunt."

The old man nodded his head. "Oh yes, the niece from the big city. How's our Phoebe doing? It's not the same around here without her."

"The doctor said she'll be fine. Thank you for asking."

His eyebrow arched. "After all of these years, what brings you to Sweet Gum, young lady?"

She glanced at Jackson. The last thing she wanted was for him to tell Harry the real reason for her visit. The fewer people who knew her plan, the better. "The timing was right with my work."

Jackson moved in closer.

Her body shivered when he placed his hand on top of her shoulder.

"Our gal Melanie is a hotshot divorce lawyer. We've got ourselves a real city slicker here, Harry."

"Very funny." Melanie shrugged her shoulder to shake off his hand. "So, what would you like for breakfast, Harry?" She pulled a notepad and pen from the pocket of her apron. As she finished taking his order, the front door flew open, and a flood of people herded into the dining area.

Melanie froze until Jackson's voice got her attention.

"How's everyone doing this morning?" He approached the hungry mob.

Melanie frowned and trailed behind him. "Where are all of these people coming from?" Pen in hand, she was ready for the rapid fire of orders.

"It's the church choir. They always come

in for breakfast on Saturday morning before practice. We have backup coffeemakers in the kitchen. You should get them going, too." He grabbed a handful of menus and passed them out to the crowd before heading into the kitchen. Melanie followed.

As she frantically started another pot of coffee, he leaned in so close she felt his warm breath on her neck. "And here you thought you could handle this on your own."

She blew her bangs out of her eyes. "Look, Jackson, I've represented hundreds of clients in highly contested divorce and custody cases. I think I can handle a few breakfast orders." She walked toward the dining area and turned. Her eyes narrowed. "The question is, can *you* keep up?"

Three hours later, feeling like she'd just run a full marathon, Melanie collapsed into a dining-room chair. She pulled her hair back and twisted it into a bun.

"Tired?" Jackson placed a glass of ice water in front of her.

He looked fresh, and she could still smell his spicy cologne. So not fair. Why did he look like the poster boy of perfection, while she probably looked like she just went three rounds in a hog wrestling competition?

She grabbed the glass and guzzled the water without stopping.

Jackson got up and brought the entire pitcher back to the table. "Maybe you'd rather drink this?" He winked and gave her a crooked smile. His piercing blue eyes held hers while she chugged another cup full.

He crossed his arms, and her eyes went straight to the biceps that were straining against his white T-shirt. "So, what did you think about the rest of the country bumpkins?"

All morning the snide comment she'd made about the horse manure and the chickens had played in her head. She'd wanted to apologize, but things had gotten so crazy. No time like the present. "Look, Jackson, we may come from different places, but I don't think you or your neighbors are bumpkins." She wiped her hands down the tops of her legs. "I'm sorry if I offended you."

He shrugged. "No offense taken." Jackson looked down and examined his fingernail. "I shouldn't have assumed you don't know your neighbors."

The truth was, she didn't know them. Her job was her world now. Actually, it had always been. She'd thought getting married and having a family would change that, but it never had. In fact, after the twins were born and she'd made partner, she'd worked longer hours.

She cleared her throat and leaned back into the chair. "You assumed correctly. I don't know my neighbors. I've been in my house for seven years, and I don't know the names of any of them." How pathetic. "They're all busy with their own lives. They don't have time to get to know each other."

Jackson wiggled in his seat. "Can I ask you something?"

Her heart raced. She wasn't ready to answer questions. "Ah…sure." As soon as she said it, she wanted to run out the door.

"Why on earth would you want to take Phoebe to a place like that? She loves people, and she'd do anything for her friends and neighbors." His face was starting to turn red. "She belongs here."

She stood and walked to the last table that held a few dirty dishes. The plates clanked when she stacked them. She turned to Jackson. "She'll make new friends. In fact, there's a senior center down the road from my house."

Jackson huffed, "A senior center? You really don't know your aunt."

Melanie snatched the forks and flung them onto the plates. "I know she's too old to be running this place." She headed toward the kitchen, and Jackson followed. She yanked the blue dish gloves onto each hand. With the water turned on full blast, she scrubbed each plate with enough force to send the yellow flower design on their surface straight down the drain. Why had she ever promised Aunt Phoebe she'd work with this man?

Jackson glanced at his watch. Fifteen minutes had passed since they'd exchanged words, and she remained in the kitchen, silent as a mouse. This couldn't continue, and he knew exactly what would clear the air. He stepped behind the counter, grabbed a carton of milk from the mini refrigerator and went to work.

"Melanie, can you come out here, please?"

The door squeaked as she exited the kitchen and walked toward him. His breath hitched as if it'd been hours since he'd last seen her. "Look, I didn't mean to upset you. Truce?" Jackson placed a glass of chocolate milk on the counter in front of her.

She placed her hands on her hips. "What's this?"

He slid into the chair at the end of the counter and patted the stool next to him. "It's only the greatest combination ever invented." He took a swig from his own glass. "Ah…whole milk and chocolate syrup. There's nothing better."

She took a seat and her lips hinted a tiny smile while she kept her eyes on him.

He tilted his head. "What's so funny? Haven't you ever seen a grown man drink chocolate milk?"

Melanie laughed. "You've got a chocolate mustache."

Jackson leaned back in his chair and crossed his arms. He'd finally gotten her to laugh. She was a tough cookie. Determined to make friends, he had to convince her to give up her idea. "That's better."

She raised her eyebrow. "What is?"

"You seem happy. You have a great laugh and your smile—it lights up your entire face. You should show it off more often."

"Sometimes there's nothing to smile about."

Jackson leaned in closer. "I have an idea."

"And what might that be?"

"Let's celebrate the end of our first day working together."

"Celebrate? How?"

"After we close, come to the fair with me— it'll be fun. We can go on the Ferris wheel."

She shook her head. "Oh no, I'm afraid of heights."

"You can keep your eyes closed."

"What's the point in going on the ride if I keep my eyes closed?"

She had a point. "Well, you can keep them shut until you feel comfortable."

"I don't think that's possible. I've always been afraid of heights," Melanie said, taking a sip of her chocolate milk. "Yum… It's really good."

"When I was a kid, I called it happiness in a glass." He smiled and took a sip from his own cup. "You know, Rebecca is afraid of being up high, too. I hope today she'll move past her fears."

Melanie swirled her straw. "It's not so easy."

He studied her face. "What?"

She held his gaze. "To move past your fears. You make it sound like it's as easy as deciding what shoes to wear."

Jackson was well aware of how difficult it was. After his ex-wife left, his fears had paralyzed him. He didn't know anything about raising a one-year-old on his own. If it hadn't been for his faith and Phoebe, he never would have survived the first year. "I didn't say it was easy. It's just doable. If you lean on God and you have supportive people in your life."

She shook her head.

It was obvious her faith wasn't as strong.

"Just don't push Rebecca if she's not ready, Jackson."

He nodded. "I won't. But I think she'll be able to conquer her fear today."

"How so?"

"She went to the fair with Mary Whiteside, and she plans to ride the Ferris wheel. Of course, that could change once she sees the size of it."

Melanie took another sip and dabbed her mouth with a napkin. "She might surprise you."

He nodded. "It wouldn't be the first time. So, what do you say? Will you come with me?"

She placed her finger under her chin. "Yes, I'll go, but I can't guarantee you a ride on the Ferris wheel."

"Never say never. Let's lock up and hit the road. First we'll swing by and check on Phoebe." His pulse sped and beat against his eardrums. The thought of spending more time with Melanie excited him, but it also had him questioning her motives. Was she being nice, or was it all an act that played into her plan? Whatever the case, an afternoon with her, outside of The Bean, put a pep in his step as they strolled into the parking lot.

Inside the truck, they fastened their seat belts. "The fair is in Harrisonburg. That's around fifteen miles from the hospital." He yanked down the visor. The sun was blinding. When he reached over to the glove compartment to grab his Ray-Bans, his hand brushed Melanie's knee. She flinched as she pulled her sunglasses from her purse and slid them on.

Jackson was anxious to learn more about Phoebe's beautiful niece during the ride. "Tell me, what made you decide to become a lawyer?"

"There was nothing else I could be." She smiled. "I come from a long line of lawyers."

"Is that so?"

"Yes. Both of my parents and all four of my grandparents were attorneys."

Jackson laughed. "Well, I guess the family was safe if anyone got into any legal trouble."

"One time when I was in high school, I mentioned to my father that I was considering becoming a doctor. You would have thought I told him I wanted to rob banks."

This was nice. He enjoyed this relaxed side of Melanie.

Her smile faded. "When my father got ill, I knew I had to go to law school. It was his dream for me, and I couldn't disappoint him. He passed away two days after I graduated."

Jackson felt her pain. "I'm sure he was very proud of you."

"I miss him."

A comfortable silence lingered before Jackson's phone rang.

They were at a red light, so he felt safe slipping the phone from his shirt pocket and looking at the screen. "It's Larry Whiteside." His heart beat a little faster. "Excuse me, but I need to take this call."

He pushed the button to answer. "Hey, Larry, what's up?"

Through the phone, Jackson heard faint music and muffled voices. Then he heard crying and knew right away it was Rebecca.

"Larry! What's wrong with Rebecca? Why is she crying? Is she hurt?"

"Calm down, Jackson. She's not hurt, but I think you need to come over to the fair."

"I'm on my way now. Can you put her on the phone?" Not being able to put his arms around her while she was obviously upset was more than he could handle.

"She won't get on the phone, Jackson."

A lump formed in his throat. "Tell her I'm coming. I'll be there as fast as I can." He ended the call, took a deep breath and then released it.

Just as the light turned green, Melanie turned and placed her hand on his arm. "Jackson, what is it?"

"It's Rebecca. Larry assured me she's not hurt, but I heard her crying." He tapped his fingers on the steering wheel. "I have a feeling she got scared on the Ferris wheel. I should have been there riding with her. I hate that she's upset and I'm not there to help her."

Melanie removed her hand from his arm. "We'll be there soon. She'll be okay."

She stared out the window while they were stopped at an intersection. She appeared fixated on the two young boys tossing a baseball in the parking lot of an antiques shop.

A large gray cumulus cloud took the sun hostage. Jackson glanced at Melanie again and saw she'd removed her glasses and was wiping away a tear that had escaped through her eyelashes.

"What's wrong?" He placed his hand on hers. "Why are you crying?"

She pulled a tissue from her purse and dabbed her eyes. "I don't want to talk about it. Rebecca needs you now."

Jackson nodded. She was right—Rebecca was his priority—but Melanie's tears worried him. When the sun emerged, Melanie put on her sunglasses once more, but he knew it wasn't to block the light.

The last few miles of the trip seemed endless. An awkward silence had filled the air after Jackson had caught her crying. She hated to get emotional in front of anyone, especially when the person was practically a stranger. Yes, he might think that he knew her, but he didn't have a clue about her life. Or the choice she made that cost her her family. If he knew the truth, that she couldn't protect her own children, he'd want nothing to do with her.

Relief took hold when Jackson zipped his truck into a grassy field, lined with cars. She sprang from the truck as though she'd stepped on a hornet's nest.

"Let me call Larry's cell phone to see where they are. Otherwise we'll be trampling all over the place." Jackson pulled his phone from his pocket.

This wasn't your normal small-town fair; there was a lot going on. She smiled at the clown who approached her, pedaling fast on a unicycle. He handed her a rose before he rode away, his red clown curls blowing in the breeze. She scanned the area, and as far as she could see, there were carnival rides, booths with various games, even a structure of some sort in the distance.

Her stomach twisted as she spied a face-painting booth. Her girls had loved to have their faces painted. A few years ago, Melanie hired a face painter for their birthday party. She could still hear their giggles. Goose bumps rose on Melanie's arms when she pictured the scene.

"Mel, are you alright? Your face is as white as a cotton field."

She pushed away the thoughts. "I'm fine."

The strap of her purse slid from her shoulder. "Did you find out where Rebecca is?"

"Wait a minute. Are you sure you're okay?"

Melanie nodded. "I just got a little light-headed, but I'm fine now." She wasn't fine. She'd never be fine.

Jackson raised a dark eyebrow. "If you feel dizzy again, let me know." He turned and walked at a brisk pace. "Larry said they're over in the food pavilion."

A small plane buzzed overhead with a banner trailing behind. Melanie couldn't make out the advertisement, but it reminded her of the planes that flew along the beach. She recalled the first time her girls had spotted a low-flying plane while building sand castles along the shore. They'd sprung to their feet, jumping up and down, pointing. "Look, Mommy," they'd both exclaimed. Wearing their matching polka-dot sun hats and white sunglasses, they'd never looked more adorable.

Melanie folded her right arm across her stomach. There were those knots again.

When they entered the food area, the sweet smell of cotton candy and funnel cake didn't do much for her queasy stomach. Mobs of people of all ages snaked through the roped-off areas in a quest for their favorite treats. She wasn't a fan of crowds.

"There's Larry." Jackson pointed toward the blue-and-yellow booth with a corn-dog sign draped across the front.

There was no sign of Rebecca, but Melanie did see a group of five grown men participating in a hot-dog eating contest. It was something she'd probably never see again.

Jackson's pace slowed when he approached Larry from behind. "Larry, where's Rebecca?" His voice trembled.

"She locked herself in the women's bathroom. Mary's been trying to get her to come out."

Melanie followed as Jackson took off running toward the bathrooms located at the back of the building. "There's Mary." Jackson pointed. "Mary! Where's Rebecca?" Beads of sweat formed on his forehead.

Mary glanced up at her best friend's father. "I'm sorry. I've tried to get her to come out. She got scared, and then some stupid older boys from our school teased her," she said, her lip quivering.

Without hesitation, he knelt and took Mary into his arms. "It's okay. This isn't your fault." Jackson stood when Larry's brother, George, approached, and Jackson made the introductions.

"It's a pleasure to meet you, Melanie, " Larry said.

Melanie offered her hand. She noticed the resemblance between the two brothers. "It's nice to meet you."

"I'll be right back," Jackson announced as he headed toward the door of the women's restroom.

Melanie grabbed his arm. "You can't go in there, Jackson. You'll frighten every woman and child inside."

His face flushed. "I guess you're right, but what am I supposed to do?" He looked up and exhaled a deep breath. "She's hurting."

Melanie's heart ached for Jackson. She knew what she had to do. "I'll go in and talk to her."

As soon as the words escaped her lips, she wanted to take them back.

What was she thinking? She couldn't do this.

He rested his hand on her arm, his eyes full of gratitude. "You would do that?"

Melanie's skin tingled under Jackson's touch. "Of course I will. I've got to pay you back somehow for rescuing me." She turned toward the bathroom with thoughts of his touch welded to her brain, along with the fear of what she'd face behind the door.

As she slowly opened the door to the restroom, her shoulders were tight. She was so nervous, and she knew exactly why. The painful memories would once again bubble to the surface, and she'd be the one in tears. How could she think she'd be any good for Rebecca? Melanie bit down on her lip and stepped through the doorway.

As she peeked around the bathroom, the bright yellow walls were blinding. Water droplets echoed from one of the two sinks. There didn't seem to be anyone inside. It was so quiet, Melanie wondered if Rebecca was even still there. Then she heard the tiny sniffles.

"Rebecca." The sounds led her to the middle stall. She gently knocked. "Rebecca, it's Miss Melanie. Will you please open the door?" This would be more of a challenge than she'd anticipated.

After a few moments of silence, the whimpers resumed.

"Please, sweetie. Your daddy's worried about you."

The lock clicked, and Melanie's shoulders dropped. One step at a time was how she'd handle it. If only she could apply that technique in her own life.

"It's okay. There's no one else here."

As the door slowly parted, relief washed over Melanie. A lump formed in her throat when she spied a little blue eye peeking through the slight opening. Rebecca stepped from the stall, her porcelain complexion covered in red splotches and her eyes puffy.

She lowered her head and rubbed her eyes. "Is my daddy here?"

There was a special bond between a little girl and her daddy. Her girls had had it with their own father, too. Many nights they demanded he tuck them into bed rather than her. An ache pierced Melanie's heart. Maybe they would have wanted her to tuck them into bed if she'd been home more often.

"Yes—he's outside." Melanie brushed her hand over Rebecca's wild blond curls, savoring the feeling. "He really wants to see you. Are you ready to go?"

She shook her head. "I'm embarrassed to go out there."

"Why?" Melanie knelt to listen.

Rebecca twirled a strand of her blond hair around her middle finger.

"You can tell me."

Her lip quivered. "This morning I told Daddy I would be brave and go on the Ferris wheel." She looked down at her fingernails. "He'll be disappointed in me."

Melanie opened her purse and pulled out a package of tissues with tiny pink carnations on the packaging. She removed one and handed it to Rebecca. "I don't think you could ever disappoint your daddy. He loves you too much."

"But he'll know I was a chicken, just like

those icky boys said." She dabbed the tissue under her nose and blew.

"Do you want to tell me about the boys?"

She gazed at the ground and scuffed her foot across the tile floor. "Those mean boys from school. They were in line behind me and Mary. They're bigger—they called me a chicken girl when I stepped out of the line." A tear slid from her eye.

Melanie took another tissue from the package and wiped Rebecca's cheek. Her hands felt clammy. How long had it been since she'd wiped a child's tear?

"There's nothing wrong with being afraid, Rebecca. Everyone is afraid of something." Being alone with Jackson's daughter was igniting fears of her own. What made her think she could help this little girl when she'd abandoned her own family?

"Are you afraid, Miss Melanie?"

After the accident, she'd lived in constant fear. The first night she'd been alone in the house, she hadn't been able to go into the master bedroom or the twins' room. For several days, she'd gathered up blankets and had slept on the floor in the dining room. Her family rarely used the room, so there were few memories to haunt her sleep. Spending time with Rebecca would only intensify the ache she felt over losing her daughters. She'd have to keep her heart closed to any emotions.

"Of course I am. I've always been afraid of heights."

A tiny hint of a smile formed. "Really? Me, too."

"I know. Your daddy told me about it earlier today." Her heart beat faster thinking about the ride. "I've never been on a Ferris wheel, either."

"You haven't?" Rebecca's small smile turned into a big grin. "Daddy's tried to get me to go on it before...but it's so high."

This little girl tugged on her heart. Rebecca's presence made her feel better than she'd felt in a long time. But she didn't deserve to feel good. "Yes, it is."

Rebecca glanced up with a serious look on her face. "It's because it goes up to heaven." She blushed. "Well, it looks like it does."

"I have a great idea." At least, Melanie thought it was. *What happens if it backfires?*

Rebecca jumped up and down. "What is it? Tell me." Her eyes lit up like lightning bugs on a warm summer evening.

Melanie reached for Rebecca's hand and led her to the sink. "I was thinking—since we're both afraid of heights, and we've never been on a Ferris wheel, what if we conquer our fear together? We can show those mean boys and your daddy we're not afraid." Melanie turned on the water and squirted soap from the dispenser.

"You mean, ride together?" Rebecca stretched her arms and held out her hands for a squirt of soap. "Today?" She looked up with dread in her eyes. She scrubbed her hands for a few seconds and reached for a paper towel.

Melanie cupped the little girl's chin and tilted her head. "Trust me, we'll be fine. As long as we're together, we can do this."

They headed toward the door, and Rebecca grabbed Melanie's hand. "Okay, let's go tell my daddy our plan."

One step at a time. That would be Melanie's mantra. Her next step, after riding the Ferris wheel with Rebecca, would be to convince Aunt Phoebe to move. Then she'd deal with everything else in her life that she'd placed in a holding pattern the past year.

With that plan in mind, Melanie felt better than she had in a long time. Then she looked down at the little girl, and the knots in her stomach returned. How on earth would she ever be able to stay away from this enchanting child?

Chapter Five

The sight of Rebecca and Melanie walking out of the bathroom nearly brought Jackson to his knees. They held hands just like mother and daughter.

"We'll wait for you over there." Larry pointed toward the lemonade stand.

Jackson nodded.

"Daddy!" Rebecca shouted and ran toward him with her arms open wide. "I missed you."

He snatched her up into a tight bear hug, never wanting to let go. When his ex-wife had told him they were expecting a child, she hadn't been happy. At first, Jackson hadn't been, either. They'd been having a rough time due to her heavy drinking. She'd promised to stop many times. And thankfully she had while she'd been pregnant. Things were good between them for a while there. But after Rebecca was born, it was back to the old Taylor. And he'd been taking care of his little girl ever since.

"Aw, sweetie, I missed you, too. You okay?"

"Those mean boys made me sad, but Miss Melanie made it all better."

Jackson turned toward Melanie. Something was different. The persistent sadness he'd seen lingering in her gaze had been replaced with a sparkle. "Thank you for everything, Melanie. I don't know what I would have done if you hadn't been here."

"Well, you could have gotten arrested for going inside the women's restroom. I doubt it's acceptable in these parts." She smiled.

He laughed. Although he enjoyed the lighthearted and funny side of Melanie, he worried about Rebecca. He didn't want her getting attached. After all, Melanie was here for only one reason—to take Phoebe away. He hoped to put an end to that idea, and she would head back to DC the way she came…alone. Still, the thought of her leaving put an ache in his heart.

He turned to Rebecca. "Can you tell me more about those boys? Do you know them?"

She shook her head. "Not really, but they go to my school. They're older and mean."

Jackson could feel the heat circling his neck. He would have liked to have been there to protect his daughter from the bullies, but he knew she'd have to learn to handle situations like this on her own. "You did the right thing by ignoring them. Let's forget about them. We're here to have some fun. Are we all ready to go on a few rides?" His daughter and Melanie eyed each other with devious smiles plastered on their faces. Something was up. "What's got the two of you grinning like you got an extra prize from the box of cereal?"

He wasn't sure what exactly had happened in the bathroom, but anything that made Rebecca look so happy was fine by him. "Is someone going to clue me in?"

"I've decided I want to ride the Ferris wheel today," Rebecca announced with a wide smile. "Miss Melanie and I are going to ride it together."

His brow arched. "Both of you—really?"

Melanie stepped toward Rebecca and reached for her hand. "We decided to conquer our fear of heights together—today." She pushed her shoulders back. "If you'd like to come along, I'm sure there's room for all three of us."

Rebecca pulled her hand from Melanie's grip and twirled two times.

Jackson laughed. "I think it's a great idea." He reached down and hoisted Rebecca onto his shoulders. "Let's go!"

Fifteen minutes later, they were all loaded

and ready to ride the Ferris wheel. Rebecca was sandwiched between her dad and Melanie, while Mary was with her father and uncle in the next cart.

Jackson glanced at Melanie and Rebecca. Both gripped the metal bar in front of them with their eyes shut tight. "Come on, girls. The ride hasn't even started."

Melanie's brow lifted, and she looked around. "Okay, I'll keep them open if you do, Rebecca."

Rebecca followed her lead and smiled. Her hands still firmly gripped the bar. "It's a deal." She glanced off to the side of the ride. Her smile disappeared.

"What's wrong, sweetie?" Jackson frowned when he saw a group of boys, probably around twelve years old, standing near the Ferris wheel. He figured they were the ones who'd teased her. "Don't let them spoil our fun."

A soft melody played, and the ride gave a slight jerk. Melanie and Rebecca squealed simultaneously.

Jackson laughed and shook his head. "You are two of a kind." He kept his eye on his daughter while their cart lifted off the ground and began slowly loading the others who waited in line.

"Daddy, I feel sick," Rebecca announced when their cart reached the highest stop on the ride.

"It's just nerves, sweetie. Once we get going, you'll enjoy the view."

She nuzzled against him and squeezed his hand. "I don't like hanging up this high."

Melanie pointed. "Rebecca, everyone looks so tiny from up here."

The little girl sat up straight and glanced around. "Those boys who teased me look like ants." She laughed and took in the view. "I think I see our house way over there, Daddy."

"I'm not sure if it's visible from here, but it does look like you can see forever." He admired the red-and-gold brilliancy surrounding them. "God does beautiful work, doesn't He?"

"He sure does, Daddy."

Jackson squeezed his daughter's hand, happy she was thankful for God's gifts. Melanie, on the other hand, remained quiet, and her body tensed at the mention of the Lord.

"You know what would make this day even better?"

"Some pizza afterward?" Jackson poked Rebecca's side.

She squirmed in the seat. "No, if Phoebe was here with us. I miss her."

He eyed Melanie. Was this how it would be when Phoebe moved to DC? "We all miss her, but she'll be home soon." If Melanie got her way, his daughter would be crushed, and so would he.

"Aunt Phoebe misses you, too," Melanie added.

Moments later, with the ride in full swing, Jackson's joy escalated at the sound of Rebecca squealing and laughing with each turn of the wheel. When Melanie joined in, it was obvious they'd overcome their fear of heights.

Back on the ground, they disembarked. Within seconds, Rebecca and Mary were jumping up and down, begging to ride again. However, this time they wanted to sit together, without any adults. After a few minutes of pleading, Larry and his brother offered to go on once more, but in the seat behind the girls.

Jackson glanced at Melanie. "How about you? Are you ready to go again?"

Melanie looked up and rested her hand across her midsection. "No, thank you. I think I left my stomach at the top." She pointed up. "Look how high it is. I can't believe you talked me into getting on that thing." She gave him a nudge with her elbow.

"Me? I didn't talk you into this. You and Rebecca cooked up this plan yourselves." He laughed. "There's a nice park over there." He pointed. "You can keep both feet on the ground."

He winked and led them toward a circle of benches with a bubbling fountain in the center.

She nodded. "Sounds good. I think I've had enough excitement for one day."

Before Melanie took a seat, Jackson watched while she reached inside her purse and pulled out some loose change. "Here, make a wish."

He smiled and took the offered currency.

Melanie closed her eyes tight as though she were back on the Ferris wheel. Her lips moved ever so slightly before she tossed her penny in.

She smiled at him. "It's your turn. Make it a good one." She looked back toward the fountain.

Jackson wasn't much for this sort of thing, but he didn't want to offend her by declining her offer. He closed his eyes and released the coin. "I guess we can't tell each other our wishes or they won't come true," he said.

Melanie stared at the water in a trance. There was sadness in her eyes. "I'm sorry. Did you say something?"

"It's nothing." He cleared his throat. "Are you okay?"

"Sure. It's just that I know I'm asking for the impossible." She walked toward the bench and took a seat, turning her face up to the sun.

He followed and sat next to her. "Do you want to talk about it?"

She nodded. "When I was little, I remember

my grandmother never passed a fountain without stopping to make a wish. I always wondered what it was that Mamaw desired so much." She paused and ran her fingers through her hair. "Several years ago, after she passed away, I was going through her things, and I found the diary she kept after my papaw died. It wasn't anything detailed, just snippets of her life, her worries and visits made by the family."

Melanie looked up at a flock of black crows squawking overhead and disappearing into the nearby woods. "Throughout her diary, she wrote about how much she missed her beloved husband. He passed away at a young age, and she never wanted to remarry. She always said he was the man God had created for her, and there was no one else."

Jackson smiled. "That's a nice thought."

"Thanks to the diary, I got the answer to my question."

"What question?" Jackson leaned in closer when a group of children ran by cheering.

Melanie tucked a strand of hair behind her ear. "What she'd always wished for at the fountains." She paused and looked way. "She wanted to be with her husband again. She didn't want to be alone."

He appreciated her openness and was actually a little surprised by it. She hadn't shared much with him about her life. He wasn't sure how to respond to her, and the silence lingered for several minutes while the sounds of birds chirping filled the autumn air. Jackson remembered the times he wished his ex-wife hadn't left, but through prayer, he discovered she'd done him and Rebecca a favor. Now all that remained were the scars. Although he missed the companionship of a woman, and he wanted Rebecca to grow up with a mother, trust didn't come easily for him. "I suppose no one wants to be alone."

He relaxed his back against the bench and watched the girls board the Ferris wheel. Now was as good a time as any to quiz Melanie a little. He puffed up his chest and released a heavy sigh.

Melanie turned. "What is it?"

"I hate to bring this up, but are you going to give up the idea to move Phoebe?" He picked at his jeans. After sharing a nice afternoon with her, he didn't look forward to the fallout from this conversation.

"Jackson, I know you love Phoebe. I also know she's been like a mother to Rebecca, especially after your ex-wife left, but she's my aunt and I know what's best for her."

Jackson stood with a jolt. "How can you know what's best? All of these years, you've never come to see her. Not once, and from what Phoebe said, all you ever do is work. When would you even have time to spend with her?" He paused and gave her a hard stare. "The people who love her most are here. She should live the last years of her life." He let out a long breath, relieved to get it off his chest. He reclaimed his seat on the bench.

"You don't know much about me or my life in DC, only what Aunt Phoebe has shared, and from what I understand, that's very little." She paused and looked up toward the puffy clouds passing overhead. "I've had a difficult time this past year. I'm not ready to share it with you now. I may not ever be, but please, I'm begging you not to stand in my way. It's best for everyone involved."

He released a defeated breath. There was no point in arguing anymore—not here. He spotted Rebecca and Mary. As they raced toward the bench, their faces beamed. He knew now wasn't the time to continue this conversation. What he needed now was a hug from his daughter. He would try to forget that Melanie was out to alter his happy family unit forever.

Monday morning was more hectic than usual. Jackson had spent twenty minutes wrangling Rebecca out of bed. Although she attended afternoon kindergarten, she'd needed to go to The Bean with her father and catch her bus there. She'd insisted today was pajama day and had refused to get dressed. When they were finally ready to leave the house, the electric garage door opener hadn't worked. If Rebecca hadn't screamed to warn him, he would have bashed right through the door.

Now, at The Bean, coffee was flowing like a river across the Corian countertop and straight onto the floor.

"Daddy! You put too much water in the machine. The coffee's going everywhere!" Rebecca announced while she placed the salt and pepper shakers on each table.

Had he filled it twice? It was possible, especially after the discussion with Melanie at the fair and the wild morning. He barely knew what end was up. Jackson raced for the mop.

Crash.

He stopped in his tracks.

"Oops. Sorry, Daddy—it just slipped out of my hand."

A mound of black pepper covered the tile floor. "Stay away from the broken glass, Rebecca. Let me clean this up first."

Jackson's shoulders tensed at the jingle of the front door bell. Why hadn't he kept the door locked? He wasn't ready for customers. The place was a mess.

"Miss Melanie! I'm so happy you're here. My daddy really needs your help." Rebecca's squeals pierced his ears.

Jackson cringed. The last thing he wanted was for Melanie to think he couldn't handle things on his own, but it was too late, the damage done. He braced himself for her scrutiny.

She glided across the floor and looked as though she'd just stepped out of the beauty salon. Her hair was perfect, her skin the color of fresh summer peaches. He scratched his head and wondered how someone could look so put together at 6:30 a.m.

"Well, I'd ask for some coffee, but I prefer mine in a cup." She grinned.

"Very funny." A slow smile came to his lips and turned into a belly laugh. He couldn't help it. He didn't know why, since they'd left things on such a sour note, but seeing her this morning made him happy. "We've kind of gotten off on the wrong foot this morning."

Rebecca skipped toward them. "Yeah, Daddy almost drove his truck through the garage door."

Melanie arched her brow. "You have had it rough." She stowed her purse behind the counter. "It's a good thing you have me to help." She winked and grabbed an apron off the hook behind the kitchen door.

She sure was cute when she wasn't fighting with him over what was best for Phoebe. He couldn't help but wonder why she was in such a good mood and so willing to help all of a sudden. Had what he'd been saying finally sunk in? He needed to know. "So, what makes you all smiles this morning?"

Melanie walked from behind the counter. "Last night, I spoke with one of my partners at the law firm. He gave me some good news about the international kidnapping case I've been working on."

His shoulders dropped. Of course she was happy about work. It wasn't because she'd changed her mind about Phoebe and knew it was the right thing to do. It was all about her job. "International kidnapping. That sounds like something from a movie."

"It's a high-profile case, and once Aunt Phoebe and I return to DC, I'll be the attorney in charge. It's a great opportunity."

Jackson walked to the sink. He turned on the water and let it run for a minute. Steam swirled up in his face as he looked over his shoulder, watching Melanie sweep up the pepper while Rebecca held the dustpan. *She thinks this is a done deal. Boy, is she ever wrong.*

* * *

Melanie carried the broom and dustpan into the kitchen. Alone, she released a loud sigh and gripped the edge of the counter. Weakness settled into her knees. Her reaction to seeing Jackson dressed in a white cable sweater with the sleeves pushed up, revealing his muscular arms, had caught her totally off guard. But it wasn't only his striking good looks that made him attractive. It was the obvious love he had for his daughter. Her heart melted, watching the two of them together. But this wasn't good. There was no time for a silly crush. She had things to take care of so she could return to her job.

With her mind preoccupied, the dustpan slipped from her hand and bounced across the floor.

"You okay in here?" Jackson poked his head through the swinging door.

Her face was hot. "Sorry... It just slipped out of my hand." She wasn't about to tell him the way he smiled at her turned her into a complete klutz. She definitely needed to get a grip.

"As long as you're okay." His head disappeared and then popped back through the door. "Maybe you should stay away from any sharp objects back there. I'm sure the pointiest tool you come into contact with at your swanky law office is a pencil." He started to close the door.

"You're quite the comedian." She placed her right hand on her hip and gave him a big eye roll. "And anyway, look who's talking. Didn't I walk into a pool of coffee? I guess the coffeemaker is too high-tech for country folk like you?"

He pushed the door wide open and gave a soft chuckle. "Actually, you might be right about that."

"Speaking of, do you want me to come out and get the coffee going? There are only ten minutes until opening, and if this morning is anything like Saturday, the herds will start to pile in any minute." She smiled and pushed her hair away from her face.

Jackson blew out a breath and nodded. "That would be great. I don't want to flood the place again." He shoved his hands into his pockets. "I seem to be all thumbs this morning. It doesn't feel right being here without Phoebe."

Simple words, yet they jabbed Melanie's heart. She knew her aunt ran The Bean primarily on her own. "I miss her, too, but I'm here, so I'll get a fresh pot going, and you can start peeling the pile of potatoes over there." She pointed to the mound next to the sink.

"Ten-four, Sergeant Harper." He did a quick salute and laughed. "Can you send Rebecca back here? I'll let her give them a good scrub."

Two hours later, the restaurant was bustling with customers. Jackson had command of the kitchen, but not without a few minor mishaps. Melanie had to use a chisel to remove the gobs of hardened egg from the skillet after he forgot to use enough cooking spray on the first batch of scrambled eggs.

Melanie thought she had everything under control until Mr. Phillips, who she learned was the town barber, requested ketchup for his eggs.

"I'll get it for you, Mr. Phillips," Rebecca announced and sprinted toward the kitchen, eager to help. She ran back out with the bottle in her tiny hands. Melanie heard the crash and watched the ketchup splatter everywhere.

"Oh no!" The woman who'd earlier introduced herself to Melanie as the pastor's wife sprang to her feet.

Melanie raced toward her. Her once-lovely winter-white pantsuit was now painted in red blobs. "Let me help you." But Melanie knew the flimsy dishcloth wasn't a solution. The suit was ruined.

Rebecca stood frozen, and then she burst into tears. "I'm sorry, Mrs. Stevenson. It was an accident." Her sobs grew in volume and traveled through the restaurant.

Jackson flew from the kitchen. "What happened? Why is she crying?"

"There was a little accident." Mrs. Stevenson pursed her lips. "No harm done. I'll go home and change before the board meeting." She snatched her purse and turned on her heel toward the door.

"Send me the dry-cleaning bill," Jackson called out before the door closed. He looked down at Rebecca.

"I'm really sorry, Daddy. I didn't mean to drop the ketchup."

No matter how hard Melanie tried to keep her feelings about Rebecca under control, her heart ached for the child.

"Okay, but try and be more careful, sweetheart."

Her head dropped, and she kicked her tennis shoe into the tile. "I will… I'll go get the mop." She shot to the kitchen.

Melanie scanned the room. Two elderly men were enjoying a leisurely cup of coffee, paying no mind to the scene that had transpired. The morning rush had finally slowed. She released a breath.

"Tired?" Jackson asked and took the mop from Rebecca. "Thank you."

"No, I'm not tired. I guess I'm not used to so much socializing at work." In DC, her day began at 6:30 a.m. She'd shut herself behind the closed door of her professionally decorated office, only to come out for restroom breaks. If she left the office after 8:00 or 9:00 p.m., it was a guarantee she wouldn't run into anyone in the elevator. That was her life.

Jackson nodded. "I suppose having your face buried in a file doesn't leave much time for talking to people."

"No, it doesn't."

The truth was that her workdays hadn't always been so bleak. She'd once enjoyed the camaraderie she shared with her fellow partners and associates. But after the accident, everything changed. The constant looks of concern and people asking how she was doing were exhausting. It was much easier to hide.

"You okay?" Jackson's light touch on her forearm brought her back to the present.

"I'm fine. I was thinking, I should probably call the hospital and see how Aunt Phoebe did last night."

"Good idea. The bus will be here to pick up Rebecca at eleven thirty. Why don't I drive you over to see Phoebe after we finish up with the lunch rush?" Jackson wiped the last of the ketchup spatters off the table.

Melanie needed to see her aunt. A shiver traveled through her body. She rubbed her arms. Talking with all the customers this morning, although they were friendly, made her feel like an outsider. "I appreciate it, but I wouldn't want to impose. I'm sure you have other things to do this afternoon."

"Nothing would make me happier than to see Phoebe, too."

She paused, but only for a moment. "Sounds like a plan, then." She retrieved her purse from behind the counter and pulled out her cell phone. "Oh shoot, my battery is dead. Can I use your phone?"

He pulled his cell from his shirt pocket. "Of course you can."

Melanie glanced at the screen and looked up. "Jackson, you have quite a few missed calls on your phone."

His eyebrow arched, and he took the phone from Melanie's hand. "What?"

"Maybe you have it set on Silent by accident."

He examined the phone. "I do. I'm not sure how it happened."

Jackson pushed the button and scrolled through calls. "This is odd." He scratched his temple.

"Is everything okay?"

"All of the calls are from an unknown number, and all within the past fifteen minutes." Jackson handed the phone back to Melanie. "Go ahead and call the hospital. It must have been a solicitor. If it had been important, the caller would have left a message."

Moments later, Melanie pushed her way through the kitchen door and into the dining area. She stopped quick and smiled. Jackson sat at a table by the window with Rebecca perched on his lap. He rubbed her curls while she quietly read to him. *Curious George.* A pain seared her stomach. It had been her girls' favorite book.

"Miss Melanie! Do you want me to read to you, too?"

Jarred back into the present, she approached the table. Her heels sounded a gentle click. "I got through to Sara at the hospital. Aunt Phoebe had a good night."

Jackson smiled and glanced at his watch. "I need to run to the store and pick up some coffee and napkins. I'm afraid we might run out before the delivery at the end of the week. Do you think you'll be okay by yourself for a bit?"

The aroma of bacon lingered in the air. The two elderly men from the morning rush had gone, and the restaurant was empty. Melanie opened up her arms. "I think I can handle this crowd." She continued to wipe down the countertop.

He motioned to Rebecca. "Come on, Squirt. Let's do some grocery shopping before your bus comes."

Rebecca sprang from her chair, leaving *Curious George* on the table. "Can't I stay here with Miss Melanie?"

Melanie ran her palm down the front of her pant leg. She enjoyed the time she got to spend with Rebecca when Jackson was around, but she was afraid of being alone with her. However, there was something about the child's disposition that made Melanie feel like she had before the accident, before her world exploded. "Yes, Jackson, please let her stay."

"Are you sure, Mel?"

"I think it's a good idea. You never know who might come in." She tousled Rebecca's curls.

Jackson jammed his hands inside the pockets of his jeans. "Okay, then. You two hold down the fort."

Melanie caught a whiff of his aftershave as he strolled toward the coatrack and grabbed his leather jacket. The hairs on her arms stood at attention. Her insides warmed at the sight of his dark hair against the leather collar. He was definitely what she and her old college girlfriends referred to as a *stud*. There was no doubt Nurse Sara wasn't the only woman in the valley who'd love the title of Mrs. Jackson Daughtry.

After a father-daughter hug, she and Rebecca waved goodbye. "Take your time. We'll be fine." Melanie's stomach clenched. Would they really be fine? She wasn't so sure. The memories of her daughters flooded her mind whenever Rebecca was around. But her adorable giggle and warm heart filled a void empty since the accident.

For the next thirty minutes, Rebecca read to Melanie as they sat at the counter. She sneaked quick peeks at the child. Joy was edging its way into Melanie's heart, and she couldn't stop it.

When an elderly couple arrived for a late breakfast, Melanie cooked scrambled eggs while Rebecca monitored the bread in the toaster. As the couple sipped their second cup of dark roast coffee, the front door bell jingled.

Rebecca hopped out of her chair and ran toward the door. "Welcome to The Bean. I'm Rebecca."

Melanie turned and spied a tall, attractive brunette standing in the doorway, looking down at Rebecca. The woman was dressed in tight blue jeans and spiked high heels, the kind you might wear to a nightclub. It was hard to tell her age from her heavy eye makeup.

She continued to stare at the little girl as though she was in a trance. A chill ran across Melanie's skin. She grabbed a menu from the counter and approached the woman. Something didn't feel right.

She extended her hand in hopes of getting the

woman's eyes off Rebecca. "Hello, I'm Melanie. Welcome to The Bean."

The woman nodded.

"You're not from around here. I know everyone." The little girl must have noticed the longing gaze the brunette was giving her, so she stepped behind Melanie in an attempt to hide.

There was something definitely odd going on, but Melanie didn't feel right chasing off a customer. "Would you like to sit at a table or the counter?"

Except for the sound of the couple's clinking silverware, silence consumed the room.

The woman glanced at Melanie, her face expressionless. Seconds later, she shook her head and exited the restaurant.

Rebecca hung on to Melanie's thigh. "Who was that lady, Miss Melanie?"

Melanie peered through the blinds and wondered the same thing. Who was she, and why did she have such an obvious interest in Rebecca?

Chapter Six

As Jackson cruised along the narrow, winding mountain road, the wildflowers' brilliant colors exploded under the autumn sun. With all the necessary supplies, he headed back to The Bean. He smiled at his recent blessings. He and Melanie were working together to keep things running for Phoebe. And Sara's report on the lady's condition was positive. Life was good. His daughter brought out a softer side of Melanie, one he found quite attractive.

He turned into the parking lot of The Bean with a tight grip on the steering wheel. Jackson did a double take when he spied a woman who resembled his ex-wife, Taylor. She was running toward a black Mustang.

His hands wet with sweat, he jammed the truck into Park. There was no way she would come back. Not now.

The engine revved and the Mustang peeled out of the parking lot, leaving Jackson's truck in a swirling cloud of dust. The high speed and the car's tinted windows made it impossible for him to get a better look.

He sprang from the truck and raced inside The Bean. His heart slowed when he opened the front door and spotted Melanie and Rebecca sitting at the counter. Each had a large glass of chocolate milk. By the looks of the dark layer puddled on the bottom, it was heavy on the chocolate.

"Well, what do we have here? Are the workers taking a break?"

Wearing huge grins, they both spun around in their stools like synchronized swimmers. "Miss Melanie made us real chocolate milk, Daddy. It's got the good syrup."

He laughed. "I see. Maybe I should have bought some more syrup while I was at the store."

Melanie smiled. "When I was a little girl, my dad let me drink it only on special occasions."

Rebecca tilted her head. "What kind of occasions, Miss Melanie?"

"If I got a good grade on my report card or did well on a test." She touched her earring. "He believed if you drank it every day, it wouldn't taste as good."

"It looks pretty tasty to me," Jackson said. He put the coffee on the counter. He was anxious to ask Melanie about the woman who'd just left the restaurant. "Hey, Squirt, why don't you go and wash an apple to take with your lunch?"

Rebecca zipped to the kitchen.

Jackson moved closer to the window. "So, did you have many customers while I was gone?"

She shook her head. "We had one really sweet couple from Upstate New York. They were on their way to Florida for the winter," Melanie said.

Jackson stepped away from the window. "Oh yes, the snowbirds. We actually get a lot of those this time of the year. Ah…anyone else?"

Rebecca poked her head from behind the kitchen door and walked toward them. "Did you tell Daddy about the strange lady, Miss Melanie?"

He noticed Melanie's shoulders stiffen, and his heart sped up. "What lady, Rebecca?" he asked.

His daughter first looked at Melanie and then at Jackson with wide eyes. "A weird lady. She didn't say anything." She shrugged her shoulders. "She stared at me for a long time. It was kind of creepy."

"What do you mean, she stared at you?"

"You tell him, Miss Melanie."

Melanie picked at her fingernail as she turned to look at him. "It was a little strange. A woman came in, but I don't think she was interested in eating or even a cup of coffee. She didn't want a table and she never said a word. She had this far-off look in her eyes and seemed confused."

"Maybe she was lost." Doubt consumed him.

Melanie cocked her head. "I don't know what was wrong with her, but she did seem captivated by Rebecca. It was very odd."

Rebecca nodded. Her curls jiggled. "Yeah, she was scary." Her nose wrinkled. "I hope she doesn't come back."

If his gut was right and it was Taylor, why would she come back after so many years away? "Don't worry. She was probably just passing through town and got lost." But until he confirmed that the "weird lady" was not his ex-wife, there was no way Jackson would leave Melanie or Rebecca alone in the restaurant.

The next morning at The Bean, Jackson was a bundle of nerves. His crazy dream from the night before, with Taylor kidnapping Rebecca, had him jumping each time the front door bell jingled. He expected to see his ex walk in and try to snatch Rebecca. To play it safe, he sat Rebecca at the far corner table, away from the door. She colored, unaware of his paranoia.

Gurgling sounds filled the restaurant when the ninth pot of coffee of the day started to percolate. He couldn't keep the pots filled. For a Tuesday morning, it was wild. A tour bus rolled in with a crowd of senior leaf-peepers. Some lingered out front to snap pictures of the golden leaves on the trees.

Thirty minutes later, Jackson stood at the window, relief settling in when the bus rolled out of the parking lot. He turned to clear the coffee cups from the table near the door.

Rebecca raised her head. "Daddy, I smell something burning." She turned her attention back to the two rabbits she chose to color purple.

He took a whiff and immediately sprinted into the kitchen. Flames shot up from the skillet. Melanie sat at a small table in the corner on her cell phone. She wrote feverously on a pad of paper, oblivious to her surroundings.

Jackson bolted toward the fire extinguisher mounted on the wall. "Melanie! There's a fire!"

With four quick blasts from the extinguisher, the fire was out. Jackson wiped the perspiration from his brow and turned toward her. Unbelievable…she was still on the phone. Didn't she smell the smoke or see the flames? She could have burned the place to the ground. He flung the skillet with the blackened bacon into the sink and stormed out of the kitchen. The crash echoed behind him.

Moments later, Melanie stomped into the dining area, carrying her phone and the pad of paper. "Jackson, I was on an important call. I didn't appreciate you banging the dishes and making so much noise."

Was she joking? She was angry at him? He bit down hard on his lip, nearly breaking the skin. "Are you kidding? Didn't you see the grease fire you started? You can't leave food cooking on the stove unattended." His anger continued to bubble.

She rolled her eyes. "Don't you think you're overdramatizing the situation? It's just a little burned bacon, Jackson."

Afraid of what he might say, he held his tongue for a moment. The rumble of Rebecca's school bus pulling into the parking lot was a relief. He'd have a few more minutes to cool off. "Rebecca, get your coat and your book bag. The bus is here."

She grabbed her stuff, ran toward Melanie and kissed her hand. "'Bye, Miss Melanie."

"Goodbye, sweetie. You have a good day."

Outside, the school bus honked its horn. Rebecca sprinted to Jackson and hugged his waist. "Please don't yell at Miss Melanie any more, Daddy. I'm sure it was an accident."

As the bus pulled out of the parking lot, Jackson turned to Melanie. "I'm sorry I yelled, but you could have burned the place down." His face pinched. "What could take priority that you'd ignore a fire?"

She looked away. "I was talking to my office."

"Ah… I should have known. Of course, your job takes priority over this hillbilly place."

"That's not fair, Jackson."

He stepped closer. "What's not fair? It's how you feel about this place…about me. I'm just some uneducated country bumpkin compared to you."

She leaned in. "For your information, my client's son was kidnapped. This case has consumed my time for weeks. The only reason my partners allowed me some time off is because I promised to work on it while I'm here."

Jackson raised his eyebrow. *Kidnapped.* Last night's dream surfaced in his mind.

Hugging the notepad to her chest, she looked him in the eye. "My client's ex-husband took their child back to his country. He went against a court order. The child has been uprooted from his home and deprived from seeing his own mother."

His anger eased. Thoughts of Rebecca filled his mind. How would he feel if Taylor kidnapped his daughter? "I'm sorry for your client and for how I acted." Who knew how much longer Phoebe would be out of commission and they would have to work together? It was time for him to accept the fact Melanie had a job back in DC. If they needed her from time to time, he'd have to adjust his frame of mind. "So, is there anything you can do for your client from here?"

"Yes, there's a lot I can do, but I'll need help from one of my partners. Still, the sooner I'm back in DC, the better." She flipped through the pages of her notes. "I'll get the child back with his mother. You can count on it."

Jackson admired her determination. He looked at his watch and realized it was already time to pick up Phoebe from the hospital and get her settled at the rehabilitation center. "What do you say if, after lunch, we lock up and go pick up our gal? If I know Phoebe, she's waiting at the front door of the hospital, wondering why we're late."

Melanie nodded and headed back to the kitchen with her head in her notebook.

Jackson watched as the door closed behind her. The fact that she was so determined made him uneasy. Of course he was concerned about her taking Phoebe to DC, but the empty feeling that consumed him when he thought about Mel leaving Sweet Gum worried him more.

Aunt Phoebe's room at Madison Village was small, but at least it was temporary. The doctor had ordered physical therapy to improve her strength, as well as speech therapy. Melanie placed the yellow mums she and Jackson had purchased on the nightstand. With the yellow-and-white comforter covering her queen-size bed, the flowers were a perfect match.

"It makes my heart happy to see the two of you came together to help me get settled." Aunt Phoebe beamed. She flung her suitcase onto the bed, not looking at all like someone in need of rehabilitation.

Jackson stepped forward. "Do you think you should be doing this, Phoebe?" He attempted to pull the suitcase away, but she gave it a tug back in her direction.

"Nonsense. I'm perfectly capable of unpacking my own clothes." She stuffed a pair of white cotton pajamas into the drawer. "Now tell me, how are the two of you getting along?" She continued to unpack.

Their eyes locked.

"The Bean is just fine, Aunt Phoebe."

"That's not what I asked, dear." She directed a knowing look at Jackson.

Melanie picked at her pant leg. She hoped he wouldn't mention the incident from earlier today.

"I guess you could say I'm great at putting out her fires." Jackson threw a wink at Melanie.

Her hopes were quashed.

Aunt Phoebe tilted her head. "What?"

Melanie closed the suitcase and shoved it into the closet. "Never mind. Jackson's just trying to be funny. Let's talk about you. Did Dr. Roberts tell you how long you'll have to stay here?" She glanced around the room, wondering if it had Wi-Fi.

"He said I'm doing well, so maybe just a week or so."

It didn't give Melanie much time to convince her aunt a move was in her best interest. With the kidnapping incident, she needed to get back to DC sooner rather than later. She'd have to start the ball rolling without Phoebe's consent. First she needed to meet with the real-estate agent she'd spoken to while she was still in DC. "That's good news. I couldn't imagine staying in this tiny place any longer than a week."

She saw Jackson scan the room. "I don't know. I think it feels kind of cozy. I guess you're used to those multilevel penthouse suites with multiple rooms and baths, and granite countertops in the kitchen."

A knock on the door prevented Melanie from getting into another war of words with Jackson. She walked to the door and yanked it open. "Hello. Can we help you?"

"Excuse me. I didn't know Phoebe had guests." A petite woman who looked about Phoebe's age stood in the doorway, holding a red spiral notebook. Her name tag read Prissy, which suited her fine with her pursed lips, pixie haircut and a sharp Adam's apple. "I'm here to take her to her speech-therapy session."

Jackson looked at Aunt Phoebe. "Boy, they don't waste any time, do they?"

Phoebe grabbed her pink sweater from the closet and slipped it on. "It's fine by me. The sooner I get all of this therapy done, the faster I'll get out of here." She turned to Prissy. "No offense, dear, but I'm anxious to get back to my own house."

Melanie's stomach turned over. It was too soon after the stroke to discuss putting Phoebe's house on the market. She'd just move forward and hope for the best. What else could she do? The stroke was proof Aunt Phoebe shouldn't be living alone, and Melanie knew there was no way she could return to DC and live alone in her big, empty house. And she had to get back. Her job was all she had left.

Chapter Seven

Late Thursday morning, Jackson watched while Rebecca safely boarded the school bus. He placed his hands on his hips and gazed toward the crystal-blue sky. He took a deep breath and inhaled the refreshing autumn air. This was apple-picking weather, but with everything going on lately, he hadn't picked a thing. That was about to change.

He jogged back into The Bean and straight to the back. He spied Melanie busy wiping down the countertops, her hair pulled back into a bun, completely oblivious to how beautiful she looked.

With the restaurant empty, he slipped into the kitchen beside her. Leaning in close, he noticed she smelled of lilacs in full bloom. "Guess what we're going to do this afternoon?"

With one last swipe of her rag, she turned her

head toward him. "Well, let's see. I've just finished the counters. Now we need to mop these floors. They're covered in grease. Then all the shelves in here need to be cleaned. We also have to pick up a few items at the store. The list is never-ending. I don't know how Aunt Phoebe handles everything."

Jackson strolled behind the counter, whistling a random tune. "All of it can wait."

A smile tugged at her lips. "It can?"

He picked up a coffeepot and scrubbed it clean while he kept his eyes glued on her. "When was the last time you played hooky and had some fun, Mel?" He turned the pot upside down on the drying towel.

Melanie crossed her arms. "Played hooky? That's for children." She rolled her eyes. "Besides, who would watch The Bean?"

"That's the great thing about being the boss... you set the hours." Jackson's heart hammered. He couldn't remember the last time he'd been this excited. The idea of spending the afternoon with Melanie had his pulse racing. "What's wrong with acting like a child once in a while?" He was long overdue for an afternoon of fun and zero responsibility.

She peered around as though someone was watching and leaned in with a smile. "What did you have in mind?"

He sauntered out of the kitchen and toward the front door. One flip of the sign and The Bean officially closed for the day. He turned to her and flashed a playful grin. "It's a surprise."

She'd followed him into the main room, and he saw she was tapping her right foot, hands on her hips. "A surprise? How will I know how to dress?"

Jackson gave her a quick once-over smile. Dressed in jeans, a crisp white blouse, she was perfect. "Trust me, what you're wearing will do just fine. Can you grab the picnic basket? It's in the pantry on the top shelf."

"Oh, so we're going on a picnic." She fiddled with her necklace. "Where are we going?"

"Would you just get the basket and quit asking questions? I need a few mustard packets out of there, too."

Melanie handed him the brown wicker basket and flashed a killer smile. Despite her earlier protest about this possibly being childish, she seemed to be on board. And maybe even looking forward to having some fun. He loaded bottles of water, a bunch of grapes and some chips. Once he'd made the turkey sandwiches with Swiss cheese on rye and wrapped them in Saran Wrap, he placed them into the basket.

"What about dessert?" She tapped her fingers along the counter. "You can't have a picnic without dessert."

Jackson spun on his heel and headed for the freezer. "It just so happens dessert is my specialty." He slid a container off the shelf and opened the lid. He pulled out two huge brownies packed with nuts and chocolate chips. "What do you think?"

Her eyes popped. "Now, that's a brownie." She licked her lips. "I've never seen ones so big."

Jackson's laughter filled the room. "It's how we make them here at The Bean—well, how Phoebe makes them." He paused. "They're not for customers. We have cakes, pies and pastries delivered. Phoebe bakes these and keeps them in the freezer for when her special friends stop in. By the time we're ready to eat them, they'll be the perfect temperature."

He tucked one of the treats into the basket. "Do you mean to tell me you've never had Phoebe's brownies?"

"No, but I can't wait to try it. Can I have a bite now?" She reached fast to snatch the second one from his hand.

He jerked his hand away and laughed. "You really are like a little kid, Mel." He tucked the brownie into the basket. "You'll get your dessert once you've eaten every bite of your lunch."

He winked and grabbed the basket. "Let's get going. I'm starved."

As they drove to the orchard, he bit his lip to keep from laughing at Melanie. She squirmed in her seat and every few minutes asked if they were there. Twice she tried to slip her hand into the picnic basket for a bite of brownie. This lighthearted side of her was driving him crazy.

Twenty minutes later, she turned to Jackson. "The suspense is killing me. Please tell me where we're going."

He smiled and hoped she would enjoy this as much as he and Rebecca always did. Rebecca's mother never liked apple picking. She claimed it wasn't good for her manicure.

Jackson hit the turn signal and pointed. "I don't need to tell you. Look over there."

She looked out the window and tilted her head. "We're going to an apple orchard?"

"It's not just any apple orchard. It's the best in the area." He pushed the button and rolled down his window. "Take a whiff of the air. There's nothing sweeter than the smell of apples ripe for the picking."

She fidgeted in her seat. "We're going to pick apples?" A silence lingered in the air. She cast a sullen look at Jackson. "I see." She nodded.

"It's a popular thing to do on a beautiful autumn day." Jackson pulled the truck into a parking space, next to the wagon used for hayrides. He slid the key out of the ignition and glanced at Melanie with an arched brow. "I'll take a wild guess you've never done this before."

The color had drained from her face. She was looking out the window as if deep in thought. "I have, but that was before…" she said in a whisper. Then, as if coming out of her trance, she turned to look at him. "I did stomp grapes once, in Italy. I was on my honey…"

"It's okay, Mel. I know you were married. I remember when Phoebe went to your wedding. You can talk about him." He reached over the console and placed his hand on top of hers. It was shaking. Was that why her mood had shifted? She was remembering her husband? "Of course, only if you feel comfortable."

"We stomped grapes while on our honeymoon." She pulled the clip from her hair and released the bun. Her chestnut mane cascaded onto her shoulders. "It feels like a lifetime ago." She gazed out the window again and watched two boys climbing onto the wagon.

Jackson leaned in. "It sounds like a lot of fun. I've never been to Italy."

She smiled. "It was messy, but so much fun. Italy is a beautiful country. If you ever get the opportunity, you should go. I'll bet Rebecca would enjoy stomping the grapes."

"Right now if a trip doesn't include a stop at Walt Disney World, she's not interested." Jackson ran his hand along the steering wheel. "She brings up the subject at least once or twice a week, usually at bedtime."

"I guess all kids would like to take that trip." A slow grin spread across Melanie's lips. "Funny, when I was little, all I thought about was becoming a lawyer. How crazy, huh?"

"I'm sure it made your parents proud." He chuckled. "What about now? Do you have any dreams?"

She shook her head. "They're for children. Plus, I think we're allowed only a certain number in our lives."

Jackson swallowed hard and let out a sigh. "So, what, you've used up all of yours? That's crazy, Mel." He shook his head. "You've got to have dreams. Otherwise, what's the point of it all?"

The quiet stretched between them.

He unfastened his seat belt and broke the silence. "Let's go pick some apples!"

She showed him the hint of a smile.

"Hold up a second." He jumped from the truck and walked to the passenger side, determined to make this day special for Melanie. He opened her door and extended his hand. As he expected, her skin was silk to the touch. Tingles shot up his arm, making him feel more alive than he had in years. She jumped at the contact and their eyes locked, but only for a second. He brushed a strand of loose hair away from her face. "Ready to play hooky?"

Melanie had to admit this beat mopping floors and grocery shopping. After an hour of apple picking, their buckets were full.

"So, are you going to bake me an apple pie with these?" He took the bucket from her hand and smiled. "Though come to think of it, you probably don't know much about making them, huh? I'm sure you buy your pies at some fancy bakery in DC."

Recalling the first time she and the girls had attempted to bake a pie jabbed a little deeper in her heart than she liked. "I've made a few, but they've never turned out right. I have trouble with the crust." She turned her face upward, savoring the warmth of the October sun.

"You can borrow my recipe if you'd like," Jackson said with a straight face.

She playfully punched his shoulder. "You don't have an apple-pie recipe—do you?"

"Sure I do. What's so hard to believe?" He glanced down toward the ground. "Well, actually it's Phoebe's recipe. She puts in extra cinnamon. Don't tell anyone. It's her secret ingredient."

"The secret is safe with me." Of course it was. She was an expert at keeping secrets.

"Let's stash these apples in the truck, grab the picnic basket and have some lunch. I know you're dying for a brownie."

As they strolled toward the truck, Melanie placed her hand on her stomach. "Actually, I am getting hungry. Do they have tables where we can eat?" As far as her eyes could see, there were rolling hills and trees dotted with yellow and burgundy under a canopy of blue sky.

"I've got the perfect spot. You'll love it." Jackson popped the trunk and dumped the apples into a large yellow cooler. He grabbed the picnic basket and a blanket then turned to Melanie. "I think we're ready. Are you up for a little hike?"

She glanced at her shoes, relieved she had on her most comfortable flats. "Sure. Lead the way."

Over a year had passed since Melanie had spent this much time outside. The four walls of her office and the courtroom were her world. A sunlit cloud drifted across the clear blue sky. After walking for twenty minutes, her mind felt clearer than it had in months. "I'm not sure why, but I feel as though I could walk forever."

Jackson stopped and looked up into the sky.

"It's because you're used to the city smog. It feels good, doesn't it?"

She wasn't sure if it was the air, the time outside The Bean or being with Jackson, but she felt so free. She raced to the top of the hill, extended her arms and twirled. "Guess who I am?" Spinning faster and faster, she suddenly lost her footing and tumbled to the ground. She pushed the hair away from her eyes and laughed.

Jackson's eyes widened. "I know that twirl anywhere. Rebecca's got a patent on it."

Melanie sat on the grass with her legs stretched in front of her. She ran her hands through the lush fescue, swallowed hard and looked up at her companion. "I can't remember the last time I sat in the grass or felt it. It's so soft."

Jackson took a seat next to her. "Can I ask you something?"

The way she felt, she was open to any question. "Sure. What is it?"

He pulled his knees close to his chest and let out a breath. "You're so good with Rebecca, and she's obviously crazy about you. Have you ever thought about having children of your own? You'd be a great mother."

Her chest constricted. Any question but this. The smiling faces of her twin girls flashed before her eyes, and hot tears blurred her vision.

When the first drop escaped, Jackson reached to brush away her tear, but hesitated for a moment. Then she felt his warm, gentle hand on her face, and a flicker of yearning bubbled inside when she realized how much she'd missed the comfort of a man's touch. "Mel, I'm sorry. Please don't cry." He plucked a blade of grass and twisted it around his finger. "It was a personal question. I'm sorry. Forget I asked, okay?"

She couldn't talk about the accident with Jackson, not now. He'd gone out of his way to make this day special for her. She wiped her eyes and sprang to her feet. "It's forgotten." Acting was what she did best. She'd been doing it for the past year. She deserved an award for her performance. "That's not necessary. I'm the one who owes you an apology, Jackson."

"For what?"

"After my car accident, you came to my rescue. I never really thanked you."

Jackson shook his head. "Yes, you did, when Phoebe and I came into your room at the hospital. You thanked me then."

That day was a blur. The one thing she vividly remembered was the moment she saw Jackson for the first time. Her heart hadn't slowed since. "Well, it wasn't much of a thank-you. And then I dropped the bomb on you about moving Aunt Phoebe. It's obvious you and Rebecca care a lot about her. I should have handled it differently."

He held up his hand. "It's all water under the bridge, Mel. We both love Phoebe, but we have different opinions on what's best for her."

"I'm beginning to think you might have a better sense of what's right."

"Really?"

Melanie closed her eyes for a moment and took in the sounds of nature. "Sometimes I feel like I don't know anything anymore."

"You know that you love your aunt."

"Yes, but—" She opened her eyes and looked at Jackson. "Do I hear water?"

He stood and extended his hand to help her off the ground. "Come with me. I want to show you something."

The moment their hands locked, she didn't want to let go. Each step led them closer to the sound she'd heard. Her heart raced. When they passed through a clearing in the thick brush, her mouth dropped at the sight of the swirling pool of angry water making a mad dash downstream.

"There she is, the Shenandoah River. It's pretty rough from all the heavy rains we've had." He held her hand tight.

"It's magnificent." She looked into his eyes. "I wish I could stay here forever." She turned back and watched the water make its journey. It was full of life and ever-changing—the opposite of her. A shiver skated down her back when thoughts of floating down the river flooded her mind. She longed to be swept away, like the raging water, to a new beginning and a new life, where she could be happy once again.

He shrugged his shoulders. "Maybe not forever, but we can have our lunch here if you'd like."

"Oh yes, please." She couldn't have thought of a better place.

Jackson carefully spread out the checkered blanket and placed the basket in the center. He bowed. "Your wish is my command."

When he took a seat, Melanie followed his lead. As Jackson unpacked their picnic, her eyes remained glued on the Shenandoah. "Can we come back here with Rebecca sometime?" A picture of her and Rebecca wading in a shallow and calmer part of the river on a hot summer day came to mind. She shook her head to erase the image. What was she thinking? She wouldn't be around during the summer. She'd be in DC, entombed in her office day after day.

"Sure, we can bring her. In fact, the apple festival is coming up soon. They have hayrides, bobbing for apples, corn mazes and other activities." Jackson handed her a turkey sandwich. "Do you want mustard?"

Melanie crinkled her nose. "Who puts mustard on turkey?"

Jackson laughed and squeezed a huge dollop onto his sandwich. "I do," he said before taking a giant bite. "Yum… It's delicious." He placed his food on the paper plate, and his eyes homed in on her.

She exhaled. The vacancy that had settled into her heart during the past year felt less daunting. Was it simply the passage of time or was it something more? She was sitting next to a man who'd gone out of his way to make an ordinary day extraordinary, just for her. She turned her face to the sun, savoring its warmth. Jackson placed his hand into hers, and her body shivered. Yes, it was something more.

Chapter Eight

The following morning, after the glorious afternoon spent with Jackson, Melanie's feet hadn't hit the ground. She wanted to bottle this feeling and take it back with her to DC.

She pulled her car into one of the last few available parking spots at The Bean. What was going on? The place looked packed. Yesterday Jackson had said it would probably be slow this morning, so she could take her time coming in. She grabbed her purse and sprang from the car. Guilt crept in at the thought of him stuck handling a large crowd alone, while she'd behaved like a lovesick woman of leisure.

The moment she stepped inside the restaurant, Rebecca sprinted toward her with her arms wide open. "Miss Melanie! You're here! I was afraid you wouldn't get here before my bus."

Melanie stooped, and Rebecca gave her a big

hug and kissed her cheek, triggering memories of her own daughters' soft lips. "What's happening here, Rebecca? There are so many cars in the parking lot."

The little girl giggled. "Everyone from town brought food." She turned and skipped toward Mary, who sat at a corner table.

She scanned the room and noticed the pastor's wife taking an order from Moe, one of the regulars. At another table, a woman she recognized from the fair poured coffee for two men.

She spotted Jackson behind the counter, wearing a huge crooked smile. Dressed in a red sweater, with a cleanly shaven face, he was busy chatting with three elderly female customers. Judging by their smiles, she figured they must think he looked as good in that color as she did. She approached him, and her stomach fluttered when she caught a whiff of his spicy cologne.

"What's going on, Jackson?"

He placed a plate of scrambled eggs in front of one of the women. He turned and their eyes connected. "Hey, Sleeping Beauty, did you catch up on your rest?" He wiped his hands on a dishrag.

Melanie opened her arms wide. "Why didn't you call me? This place is buzzing like a beehive."

She took a seat at the counter, and he slid

a glass of ice water in front of her. "We had a minor problem when I opened up." He moseyed down to the end of the counter and poured a cup of coffee for a young man who'd just sat down. Jackson passed him a menu and returned to their conversation. "When I arrived, the stove was acting a little funny."

"Funny? How so?"

"Well…it broke."

"What? Why didn't you call me? This isn't a minor problem, Jackson. It's a disaster. This place is Aunt Phoebe's livelihood."

"Relax, Mel." He took a swig of his coffee. "We've got it all under control."

"How?" Her jaw tensed.

"Fred Johnson came in first thing, hungry for a stack of pancakes. When I told him the stove wasn't working, he'd left in a huff. My guess, he told his wife, Clarice. She likes to spread news, if you know what I mean." He chuckled. "People from town brought every item on the menu."

"What?" Her heart softened. She looked out the window and tried to hide tears that pricked her eyes.

Jackson reached across the counter and rested his hand on hers.

Melanie bit her lip. "So they spent their hard-earned money, and now some are here working for free?"

With his hand still on hers, he leaned in with a smile. "This is how it is in a small town, Mel—well, at least in Sweet Gum. People do for one another. That's what makes it such a wonderful place to live and raise a family. People in the valley help those in need. It's what God's called us to do." He looked around The Bean and smiled.

Melanie scanned the room, and a chill traveled through her. "All of these people are here to help my aunt Phoebe." This would never happen in a big city like DC.

"Yes, we all love Phoebe, and in this town, you take care of the ones you love."

His words jabbed straight to her heart. If she'd lived here when her family was killed, would she have lived an entire year in isolation? No. These kind people would never have allowed that. They would have rallied around her just like they were doing for Aunt Phoebe. And Jackson, he'd dealt with the problem on his own so she could get some rest.

Her stool screeched along the floor as she pushed her way from the counter and walked into the kitchen. She grabbed an apron hanging on the hook next to the pantry. Securing the strings around her waist, she returned to the dining room. She gazed across the floor, watching the townspeople hard at work. The love in the room exploded beyond the walls of The Bean. Then reality hit. Why would she want to take all of this from Aunt Phoebe?

By the time Rebecca caught the bus later that morning, the stove was up and running, thanks to the town's handyman. Melanie stood at the corner table, taking an order. Jackson smiled at the sound of Melanie laughing, something she seemed to be doing more of lately. He hoped he was part of the reason behind her happiness.

With his view obstructed, Jackson was unable to see who was making her laugh. She certainly was enjoying herself.

With a wide smile covering her face, she glided across the dining-area floor and stopped at the coffeepot. "Is there fresh coffee, Jackson?"

Great, now he could sneak a peek at the customer. He bit his lip when he spied a man with blond hair and a dark tan. Jackson's pulse raced. The man making Melanie giggle like a teenager with a crush looked young and muscular. Jackson's brow furrowed when he noticed a few female members of the small tour group staring and whispering. What was it about this guy?

"Jackson, I asked if there was fresh coffee."

"You're sure in a good mood." Jackson handed her the coffeepot. "I don't think I've ever heard you laugh so much." He crossed his arms on his chest. "Who's the guy? He's not a local."

Jackson knew everyone in Sweet Gum. Did Melanie know him from DC? Maybe he was some hotshot lawyer from her firm. One thing Jackson knew for sure—he got his tan from a bottle.

Melanie smirked. "Why, Jackson Daughtry, are you jealous?"

"Jealous? Of course not. I just think you'd better be careful. I've known plenty of guys like him."

"Like what, handsome and successful?" She turned on her heel and headed back to the stranger's table.

There was no way he was jealous. Was he? He clenched his teeth. Inhaling a deep breath, he grabbed the other pot of coffee and bolted to the table next to Melanie. As he refilled the coffee cups of two women, he strained to hear what Melanie was saying, but all he heard were more giggles. Who was this guy? Some sort of comedian?

Jackson turned with a jerk. "Excuse me, Melanie, but I need to speak with you in the kitchen."

She spun around, and her hair whipped over

her shoulder. "One second. I need to take Richard's order." She took a seat next to Richard.

So what, now she was going to have a cup of coffee with the guy? She scribbled something on the back of an order ticket and slid it across the table. Did she just give him her phone number? Every muscle in Jackson's body tightened. Was he asking her on a date?

Jackson wasn't sure what was going on, but the emotions that erupted were something he hadn't experienced since high school. Melanie was right. He was jealous.

Melanie couldn't believe it. The handsome Jackson Daughtry was jealous. Her heart fluttered at the thought. While she cleaned out the last coffeepot, she recalled the tense expression on his face while she'd spoken to Richard.

"Well, it's almost two. Looks like we're finished for the day," announced the man who'd been taking up most of her thoughts lately as he turned the sign at the front door to Closed.

She looked away for a moment. They'd visited Aunt Phoebe together the last couple of days. It was understandable Jackson assumed they'd go today, too, but after his reaction to Richard, Melanie wasn't sure if he'd ask. She cleared her throat. "I can't go today, Jackson." The dishwasher kicked into the rinse cycle. "I've got a few errands to run."

His shoulders slumped. "Oh...okay." He turned and grabbed his jacket. "Maybe I'll go ahead and visit her. I have some pictures of Sam and Rebecca I wanted to give to her."

"I think she'd like it." Melanie's voice cracked.

He gave a half smile. "I think so, too."

The shrill of the telephone behind the counter caused Melanie to jump. Jackson walked toward it and answered on the second ring.

"Thank you for calling The Bean. This is Jackson." He ran his fingers through his hair once and then again. "Hello. Is anyone there?" he snapped. "Hello!" He paused for a second and slammed the phone back on the hook.

"Nobody there?" Melanie reached for her purse and swung it over her shoulder.

"It's hard to tell. I thought I heard someone breathing, but the line sounded dead." Jackson frowned. "So, you're heading out for your errands?" he asked as he strolled toward the coatrack and slipped on his jacket.

Her face warmed. *Gosh, he looks good in leather.* "I'm sorry I can't go with you to see Aunt Phoebe. Maybe I can meet you over there later."

He nodded. "I'd like that." He tossed a grin

over his shoulder as he headed toward the door. "Let's go."

With legs like overcooked spaghetti noodles, she followed him to the parking lot. If he only knew where she was going, he'd change his mind about meeting later.

Fifteen minutes later, as Melanie sat on the front porch of Aunt Phoebe's house, she took off her jacket. Despite the crisp air, the autumn sun felt more like August. She rubbed the back of her neck as she spied a deer grazing along the property line. Before Richard left The Bean, he said he'd meet her by two thirty. She glanced at her watch. He was late. A thickness formed in her throat. There was a part of her that wished she'd never arranged this appointment before she'd left DC. Seeing the town come out to help her aunt had been a curveball she hadn't expected. She'd give him another few minutes before she headed to the rehab facility. Her pulse quickened at the thought of spending more time with Jackson outside The Bean. Their day together at the orchard was the first time since losing her husband that she'd considered a relationship with a man. But what would she do? Move to Sweet Gum? Her job was in DC. Her heart shrank.

Minutes later, Richard's candy-apple-red Corvette tore up the gravel driveway, scaring two squirrels up a nearby oak tree. Funny, the real-estate agents she knew typically drove a car with a backseat for clients.

"I'm sorry I'm late." He took off his jacket and tossed it inside the car. "Let's get the tour started." He slammed the door, and they headed inside.

Down in the basement, Richard checked out the age of the hot water tank while Melanie took notice of the stacks of boxes lining the wall. Aunt Phoebe sure had a lot of stuff. This move would be a tremendous undertaking. Why had she kept this appointment?

Richard walked toward her and wiped his hands down the front of his slacks. "The tank looks brand-new. Potential buyers like new."

As they headed up the stairs, Melanie could have sworn she heard someone walking around in the house. "Do you hear something?"

He stopped at the top of the stairs. "Wait here."

Melanie froze. Why had she left the door unlocked? Then again, who would think about crime in this friendly town?

She tiptoed to the top of the stairs and put her ear to the door. Richard spoke to the intruder, but it wasn't a prowler. She recognized the voice and burst through the door. "Jackson, what are you doing here?"

Both men jumped.

"I could ask you the same thing, Mel." His eyebrow rose. He looked at Richard and then took a couple of steps toward her. "I thought you were running errands." His eyes narrowed. "What exactly is going on here?"

Melanie shrugged. "I asked you first. What are you doing here? You're supposed to be visiting Aunt Phoebe."

Jackson took a step back. "I came here first to pick up her laptop. When I called to let her know I planned to stop by, she asked if I could bring it to her."

"Oh, I see." Melanie glanced toward the floor. She braced herself for Jackson's reaction when he found out why Richard was at Aunt Phoebe's house.

"So, are you going to tell me what's going on? Why you're here with him? Alone?"

She and Richard looked at each other, and then he turned on his heel and headed toward the front door. "I think I'll leave you two alone. I'll be in touch, Melanie." Within seconds, she heard Richard's car race down the driveway faster than it had arrived.

Jackson placed the laptop on the foyer table and crossed his arms. "Boy, he's sure acting guilty." His eyes were sad. "What's up, Mel?"

She swallowed the lump in her throat. It was

time to come clean. "He's a real-estate agent, Jackson." Saying it out loud made everything so real and very wrong.

His sad eyes quickly turned to anger. "Does Phoebe know you've got an agent looking at her house? This will crush her."

Her breathing accelerated. Why did Jackson have to show up? He was going to ruin her plan, but maybe it should be ruined. She headed toward the kitchen for her jacket and purse. "He's just looking. It's not like he's going to stick a For Sale sign in her yard today."

Jackson followed close behind. "You didn't answer my question. Does Phoebe know about this meeting?"

"No, she doesn't know, but it's not a big deal—it's just a meeting."

"It does matter, Mel. You're going behind her back." He looked up at the pendant light when it flickered. "It's deceitful."

She grabbed her coat off the back of the chair and jammed her arms into the sleeves. "It's family business, Jackson, and I'd appreciate it if you didn't mention it to Aunt Phoebe today." She swung her purse over her shoulder, nearly hitting him in the chest.

Melanie couldn't get out of there fast enough. She raced out the front door, trusting Jackson would lock up the house. She pitched her purse

into the backseat, and its contents went flying.
When she crawled into the backseat to retrieve
the lipstick tube that rolled under the passenger
seat, she felt something soft and fuzzy. It was
stuck way underneath the seat. She was never
good about cleaning her car. Her husband used
to tease her about it. She reached farther with
only her fingers touching. With a swift yank,
she came face-to-face with Joey, the twins' favorite stuffed animal. The day she'd given it to
them, they'd asked why she hadn't bought two.
She'd sat them on the couch and told them the
importance of sharing.

Melanie buried her face into the animal and
wept. Why was Jackson making this so difficult? And why was this town tugging at her
heart, making her doubt her plan? She wanted
her old life back—or did she want this new life
that was slowly growing on her?

She settled back into the driver's seat and
rested her head against the steering wheel. Her
chest squeezed. *What are you doing?* She took
a deep breath and exhaled before putting the
car into Drive. As she pulled away she glanced
at the rearview mirror. Jackson was at the window, looking as though he'd lost his best friend.

Her stomach was queasy. Going behind
Aunt Phoebe's back to sell her house had been
wrong. She knew it. Since losing her family,

she'd felt threatened by her own fear of being alone. Rather than face it, she'd cowered like a dog during a thunderstorm. No more. She knew what she had to do.

Chapter Nine

Melanie headed to the rehab center, her eyelids heavy. Her conversation with Jackson whirled through her mind. *Deceitful.* He was right. She was doing whatever she had to in order to make herself feel better. When she caught a glimpse of Ackerman's General Store, she hit the turn signal and pulled into the parking lot.

In anticipation of a much-needed caffeine jolt, she raced through the door and straight to the glowing sign that read Pepsi. She snatched a bottle and twisted the lid, releasing the fizzing sound. She drew the bottle to her lips and took an extended pull from the bottle. After the fiasco at Aunt Phoebe's house, her nerves were frazzled.

She scurried toward the front of the store and grabbed a pack of Altoids along the way. As she neared the register, she stopped dead in her

tracks. There, standing in front of the news-
stand, reading a paper, was Richard. At first she
wanted to turn and hide. Instead she swallowed
the bulge in her throat and headed straight toward him.

Richard turned at the sound of her heels clicking along the oak floor. "Melanie, what a surprise. Are you ready to list the house?"

The cold soda warmed inside her sweaty
palm. "Not exactly."

"What does that mean?"

A dull ache throbbed between her eyes. "I've
changed my mind. I'm not going to sell Phoebe's house." Her shoulders relaxed at her words.

A chuckle rumbled from his throat. "You're
kidding, right? You seemed so determined when
we spoke while you were in DC."

"I've just changed my mind—that's all."

He cast her a sullen look. "Well, it's all for the
best. It was obvious you'd upset that guy. But
from what I could see, he probably won't stay
mad at you for too long."

Melanie could only hope Jackson would for-
give her. She'd been so wrong. "I'm sorry I've
had a change of plans."

A smile flickered at the corner of his lips. "It's
all part of business. Who knows? Maybe I'll be
looking for a house for you and that guy—Jack-

son, wasn't it?" He winked and turned toward the door.

Her breath quickened at the thought of a life with Jackson and Rebecca. Could that ever happen? She knew she'd first have to convince Jackson that she wasn't truly selfish, just scared. But the thought of revealing the reason for her fears scared her even more.

Hearing a knock at Phoebe's door, Jackson got up to answer and came face-to-face with Melanie. After he'd caught her with the real-estate agent, he'd been fuming. He'd finally cooled off, but seeing her again sent his pulse racing. It wasn't just because of what happened at Phoebe's house. It was the way she looked standing in the doorway, with the light from a nearby window putting her in the spotlight. Her hair was tousled from the stiff breeze that had picked up during the day. She looked beautiful, and no matter how hard he tried, he couldn't stay mad at her.

Phoebe stood up from the Kennedy rocking chair that sat in the corner of her room. "Hello, dear. I wasn't expecting you so soon. I thought you had errands this afternoon."

Jackson leaned in, curious to hear how Melanie would answer. He watched while she twisted a strand of hair around her finger.

"I really wanted to see you," Melanie responded, squeezing Phoebe's hand. "The errands can wait." Her eyes darted toward Jackson.

She looked cute when she was nervous, like a child who'd been put into time-out. She probably thought he'd told Phoebe about the incident at her house. He could never do that, especially since Phoebe was still recovering. Why upset her? He intended to nix Melanie's plan to list the house on his own. Phoebe would never have to know.

"How sweet. I was just speaking with Jackson about a favor I need from him. I hate to ask since you've already done so much."

Jackson shook his head. "Phoebe, I told you, it's not a problem." When his cell phone chirped, he pulled it from his shirt pocket, but the caller had already hung up. The display indicated another unknown call. This was getting old. He jammed the phone back into his pocket.

Melanie glanced at Phoebe. "What's going on?"

"It's no big deal. She has some old furniture she's donating, and it's scheduled to be picked up at her house today," Jackson explained.

"Is there anything I can do?" Melanie asked.

"You can stay here and visit with Phoebe." Jackson glanced at Phoebe and checked his watch. "What time are they coming?"

Phoebe opened the drawer of her nightstand and pulled out her day planner. "Oh, I've made a mistake."

"What's wrong, Phoebe?"

"I thought I had it scheduled for five, but it's actually three thirty. You have to pick up Rebecca."

Jackson scratched his head. That wasn't good, but he didn't want to disappoint Phoebe. "I'll call the Whitesides' house and see if Rebecca can go home with Mary." He reached for his phone.

"Can't I meet the driver, Aunt Phoebe?" Melanie suggested.

She shook her head. "I appreciate the offer, but there's some heavy furniture. It will take two men to get it out of the basement and onto the truck."

Melanie turned to Jackson. "I could pick up Rebecca for you, if you're comfortable with her riding in the car with me."

Phoebe clapped her hands together. "I think it's a terrific idea. Don't you think so, Jackson? You know Rebecca is crazy about Melanie."

He was well aware of the growing attachment between Melanie and his daughter. After Melanie's secret meeting with a real-estate agent, Jackson was even more determined to prevent the move. He knew if he allowed Melanie to pack up Phoebe and head back to DC, Rebecca would be heartbroken. For now, he wanted to keep his commitment to Phoebe. Against his better judgment, he answered Melanie. "Why would picking up Rebecca make me uncomfortable?"

Melanie pulled a notepad from her purse and handed it to Jackson. "Write down the school's address. I'd be happy to pick her up."

He scribbled the address into the notepad. "I really appreciate this, Mel." He smiled. "Sometimes it's hard being a single dad." Rarely did he admit it to others. He prayed for guidance, but it was a struggle he usually shared only with God.

He handed the notepad to her. Their fingertips brushed, and something stirred inside him.

"I'm sure it is, Jackson."

A warmth coursed through his body, catching him off guard. Even more unsettling was the fact that it hadn't been the first time. He couldn't fall for her. She would eventually go back to her life, leaving Rebecca longing for a mother figure and Jackson wondering what could have been.

He had to drop these crazy fantasies of him and Melanie together as a couple. "Okay, so you'll pick up Rebecca and bring her back to

Phoebe's house. It shouldn't take us more than a half hour to load the truck."

Jackson took out his cell to call the school. When a nonfamily member picked up a child, they required notification before the pickup. He stepped toward the door to make the call.

"I'm sorry we won't be able to visit for long today." Melanie reached for Phoebe's hand.

"It's alright, dear. I have physical therapy scheduled at three thirty."

"How's it going? Can you tell if you're regaining your strength?"

"She'll be back at The Bean, bossing everyone, before we know it." Jackson stepped back into the room. "Nothing keeps her down."

Phoebe laughed. "Not if I can help it. I'm already making progress. The therapist said if I continue to show improvement, I could be released within the next week. I'll be happy to get home, although I will have to continue treatments there for at least a couple of weeks."

Jackson smiled. Perhaps he'd have more time to change Melanie's mind. "Well, you'll be in your own space. That's what counts." He eyed Melanie. "It's terrific to live in a small town where everyone cares about you. You'll have the entire population waiting on you."

Phoebe smiled. "You're right, Jackson. I'm

blessed to live in a place with such caring people." She looked at Melanie. "You see, dear, I could never leave the valley."

"I think Melanie has to spend a little more time here. She'll realize that once you come to the valley and meet its people, you never want to leave." He reached into his pocket and pulled out his keys. "I'd better get going." He turned and swallowed hard as he gazed at Melanie. "Thanks for picking up Rebecca, Mel." He pulled the door closed before she responded.

He'd called her Mel. Would he have called her that if he'd still been angry? The sooner they could have some alone time and she could talk to him, the better.

"That young man is crazy about you." Aunt Phoebe closed the drawer and took a seat in her rocking chair.

Melanie ran her fingers through her tangled hair. "I don't think so." She paused. "He's actually upset with me right now."

"That's impossible. I can see it in his eyes. He cares about you so."

She walked toward her aunt's bed and took a seat. "Something happened this afternoon, but I don't want to go into the details—not now." She stared at the ground. "What I do want to tell you is that I've changed my mind."

Aunt Phoebe gave her a questioning eye. "About what?"

Melanie lifted her head and nodded. "I'm not going to move you back to DC with me."

"I'm happy you've finally realized this is where I belong."

Melanie folded her arms across her chest. "Where do I belong?"

Her aunt pushed herself out of the chair and walked toward her. She reached out and took hold of her niece's hands. "Perhaps you should ask God that question, dear."

Melanie's entire body tensed. "I don't think God is listening—at least, not anymore."

"Believe me, He'll listen if you have faith. He'll answer your question, but I think you already know the answer. You must pray for discernment." Aunt Phoebe gave a nod, and a slow smile spread across her lips.

Melanie stood and embraced her only living family member. The tears began to flow, releasing all of the pain she'd held on to the past year. The fears that had kept her in bondage were slowly losing their grip. "As much as I want you with me, it was all for selfish reasons. I know this is where you belong." She didn't want to let go. In her aunt's arms, she felt safe. When a ray of sun crept through the lace curtains and kissed the side of her face, she knew it was time to choose faith over fear.

Chapter Ten

Twenty minutes later, Melanie cruised into the carpool lane at Rebecca's school. She was early, but still several cars back in the line. As she waited for Rebecca, she felt at peace in ways she'd never imagined. She'd lived the past year numb, experiencing the first everything since the accident—birthdays, holidays and anniversaries. In the end, life had continued.

She knew now she'd have to make the accident a part of her life. She could move on and take steps to rebuild her life. It would take time, but she was hopeful.

Her heart raced at the sound of the bell. She smiled when she saw all the children buzzing out the door like a swarm of honeybees. Their tiny legs barely kept up with the rest of their bodies.

Smiling, she continued to watch the children.

Her smile faded when she saw twin girls with the same coloring as her girls. She couldn't breathe. What happened to her air? And the calm she felt only moments earlier? Frantic, she pounded on the button to roll down her window, but it failed to open. She grabbed the door handle and sprang from the car. She bent over, her head down and her hands on her knees. Her world spun out of control.

"Miss Melanie, Miss Melanie."

The spinning stopped at the sound of Rebecca's sweet voice. As she felt the warmth of the tiny hand on her cheek, the panic eased.

High heels tapped along the sidewalk. "Miss, are you okay?" Holding a portfolio in her arms, a young, petite redhead placed her hand on Melanie's back. "I'm Rebecca's teacher, Susan Murray. Do you need me to call someone?"

Melanie reached for Rebecca's hand. This was all she needed. Since the accident, no one touched her in the way this child had. "Oh no, I'm fine." She looked down at Rebecca. "I'm sorry if I frightened you."

The little girl pushed her curls off her face. "It's okay, Miss Melanie." She giggled. "I thought I'd have to call my daddy to rescue you again."

Melanie wasn't surprised by the calming effect Rebecca had on her. Over time the child had gone from being the cause of her panic to being the cure. And it wasn't just her. Despite their dispute over Phoebe, Jackson was proving to be a balm to her battered heart, as well. Like taking her on that picnic. He'd sensed how tightly she was wound up and had wanted to bring her just a little joy.

Melanie wondered if both Rebecca and her daddy could liberate her from the isolated life she'd built for herself. From the crushing melancholy she'd been grappling with since the accident.

Miss Murray motioned to the cars behind Melanie to go around, and the carpool line began to move at a snail's pace. "Mr. Daughtry called to let me know you planned to pick up Rebecca." She examined Melanie's face with her brow raised. "Do you think you're okay to drive?"

"I'm fine. I think I had the heat up too high in the car. I started to feel warm." She couldn't tell by the look on the teacher's face if she believed her story or not. "I also had way too much coffee today and not enough water," she added.

Rebecca glanced up at Melanie. "Daddy always says it's important to drink lots of water."

Melanie cupped the child's chin. "Your daddy's a smart man." She picked up Rebecca's backpack from where it was resting at her feet. "So, are you ready to go?"

"Yes! Yes!" Rebecca began her signature twirl. Melanie and the teacher broke out into laughter.

As Miss Murray walked back toward the school, Rebecca dropped to the ground. Dizzy from twirling, she giggled and grabbed for her lunch box.

Melanie extended her hand to help her up. She noticed Rebecca's smile disappeared. "What's wrong?"

Her face pale, Rebecca pointed across the parking lot. "It's the lady who came to The Bean, Miss Melanie." Her eyes were like saucers. "Remember, the one who stared at me." She turned with a jerk and buried her face into Melanie's stomach. "Make her go away, please."

The woman continued to watch them.

"Is she gone yet?" Rebecca asked with her face still covered.

Like the protective mama bear, Melanie had no other option. Every muscle in her body was tense. She threw her shoulders back and made eye contact with the woman. "I'm going to call the police if you don't leave," she yelled across the grounds.

"Are you really going to call the police, Miss Melanie? Will they put her in jail?"

Melanie watched as the woman dropped her head and turned. She walked to the far parking lot and climbed into a car. Who was she? And what did she want?

She dismissed the questions about the odd woman. It was probably all a coincidence. What else could it be? Inside the car and buckled up, Melanie headed toward Aunt Phoebe's house.

"Did you have a good day at school?" She eyed Rebecca in the rearview mirror. Melanie noticed she wasn't wearing her normal smile. "Is everything okay?"

"No. I have a problem," she whispered while she stared out the window.

"Do you want to talk about it? Maybe I can help." Melanie wasn't sure what kind of problem could have developed in the few hours since she left The Bean to go to school, but how bad could it be? She was only five.

She squirmed in her seat. "Daddy won't be happy. I forgot to give him the note from my teacher last week."

"I'm sure it will be okay. Do you know what the note said?" She couldn't imagine Rebecca misbehaving in class. Of course, every child slipped up now and then.

"Well, each month Mrs. Murray has a birthday party for all the kids who have birthdays that month. Tomorrow we're celebrating all the October birthdays."

"That sounds like fun." The back of Melanie's seat started to vibrate. "Try not to kick the seat. Why do you think your daddy will get upset?"

"Monday's my turn to bring in the cookies. I had a note from Mrs. Murray so we'd have plenty of time to bake. She knows how busy Daddy is. I forgot to give it to him last week." Rebecca let out a weary sigh.

Busy didn't begin to describe Jackson's life. Raising a child on his own couldn't have been easy. And since Aunt Phoebe's stroke, he was using his vacation time to cover at The Bean. She wondered how he managed to do it all. She wanted to do something to help him.

She also wanted to make up for upsetting him by meeting with the real-estate agent.

She knew just the thing.

Melanie whipped the car into the parking lot of the market where she'd stopped earlier. She put the car into Park, unbuckled her seat belt and turned around. "Don't worry. I have an idea."

"You do? What is it?" Rebecca asked, wearing a Christmas-morning smile.

She pulled her cell phone from her purse and pushed the speed-dial button that read Hero. Of course, she'd have been mortified if Jackson or anyone knew this, but in her eyes, he was a hero. He not only had rescued her the day of the accident but also was going beyond the call of duty to help keep The Bean open for Aunt Phoebe.

"Who are you calling, Miss Melanie?" She peered over the seat. "Hey, you have one of those old phones just like my daddy."

"You're right, and that's exactly who I'm calling. You and I are going to bake those cookies together…just the two of us."

Rebecca bounced up and down in the backseat. "Yippee!" the little girl yelled as Jackson answered his phone.

"Well, I certainly don't get that kind of reaction from Rebecca when I drive her home from school." Jackson chuckled. "What's up, Mel?"

"Would you mind if we stopped by The Bean instead of coming over to the house?" She took a swig from her bottle of water.

"Of course not. I'm still waiting for the guy to pick up the furniture, so take your time. But why are you heading there?"

A picture of her and Rebecca in the kitchen baking cookies together flashed in her mind. A sense of peace took hold. She recalled many rainy Saturday mornings when she and her daughters had done the same. The kitchen had always been full of laughter. "Rebecca and I plan to do a little baking. Her class is having a party on Monday, and it's her turn to bring in the cookies."

Jackson laughed. "Let me guess. She showed you a note from Mrs. Murray that she should have given me a while back?"

Melanie chuckled, even more impressed with Jackson and his relationship with Rebecca. "You know your daughter too well, Jackson."

"Yes, I guess I do. Obviously this isn't the first time she's done this. We're trying to work on her organizational skills."

"She'll grow into it. She's still a little girl." Melanie remembered her own daughters. Alissa had been so structured and organized, while Alina had been all over the place.

"I know, but sometimes I wish she would stay this young forever, Mel."

In the background, Melanie heard a loud knock at the door. "I guess you have to go?"

She didn't want to end the call. She was enjoying their conversation, but he had work to do, and she was sitting in a parking lot. "I'll bring Rebecca home when we're done, if it's okay."

"I was thinking, before we go and eat, we could take Rebecca to visit Sam. Why don't I come by The Bean when I'm finished here? We can head over to see the puppies and then grab a bite."

"It sounds like fun. I appreciate you letting

me tag along." Her heart soared. "So, we'll see you in a few hours." She ended the call, but her feelings for this warm and handsome man lingered.

Rebecca leaned over the front seat and rested her chin on the back of Melanie's leather seat. "Is he mad at me?"

She found it endearing that Rebecca didn't want to upset her father. Melanie had been the same when she was a little girl. Even as she went off to college, she lived for her father's approval. "No, he's not upset at all. In fact, he said it was okay for us to bake the cookies together at The Bean. After he's done at Aunt Phoebe's, he'll come over, and we'll go see Sam and then grab some dinner." She ran her hand through Rebecca's blond ringlets. The feel ignited memories. "How does that sound?"

"It sounds like the best day ever!"

Melanie pulled the key from the ignition and removed her seat belt. Rebecca's enthusiasm was invigorating. "It sure does. What do you say we go and start the fun?"

After ten minutes of deciding between chocolate-chip and snickerdoodle cookies, Rebecca finally made up her mind. They'd bake chocolate-chip cookies for the class and snickerdoodles for Jackson, since they were her daddy's favorite cookies. With all the ingredients in the shopping cart, they were ready to check out at the register.

"Look, there's Mrs. Stevenson." Rebecca pointed toward the register.

"Oh yes, it is." She tried to stall, but Rebecca took off running. Her pink tennis shoes with tiny rhinestones on the side sparkled.

Melanie bit hard on her lip. Running into Mrs. Stevenson while with Rebecca would raise questions about her relationship with Jackson that she wasn't sure she was ready to answer.

"Rebecca, it's nice to see you. Where's your daddy?"

"He's at Phoebe's house, moving furniture." Rebecca answered while she clutched a bag of marshmallows to her chest.

Melanie peeked through the loaves of bread and saw the arch of Mrs. Stevenson's eyebrow. "You're not here alone, are you?"

She was tempted to linger in the bread aisle, but it was too late. And besides, why was she hiding? There was nothing wrong with her being here with Rebecca.

Melanie stepped from the aisle and was face-to-face with Mrs. Stevenson. "Of course she's not here alone." She swallowed hard. "She's here with me. We're baking cookies, and we needed a few ingredients." There, she'd said it. Now she wanted to run from the store, run from the valley and all the people she was beginning to care about far too much.

An enormous smile formed on Mrs. Stevenson's face. "It's so nice of you to help Jackson."

"After me and Miss Melanie finish baking, Daddy's picking us up at The Bean. We're going to see my new puppy, and then we're going out to dinner. It will be the best day ever."

"Oh…how nice." She smiled at Rebecca and turned her attention to Melanie. "It's good to see Jackson dating again. He doesn't make enough time for himself."

Melanie's stomach lurched. This was exactly what she'd been afraid of. She could hear the wheels spinning in Mrs. Stevenson's head. It was clear she liked to talk around town. She needed to nip this in the bud and fast. Thankfully Rebecca beat her to it.

"It's not a date. I'll be there, too. If it was a real date, Daddy would pick up Miss Melanie in his truck and bring flowers," Rebecca stated with innocence.

Thoughts of Melanie's first date with Jeff filled her head. He'd picked her up in his 1979 Datsun and brought her pink calla lilies.

Mrs. Stevenson smiled at the little girl and turned to Melanie. "Well, perhaps a real date will be in the future. I think you and Jackson have more in common than you realize."

Rebecca had wandered over to the candy aisle before she heard Mrs. Stevenson. Melanie wanted to pay for the groceries and leave before her little ears picked up on Mrs. Stevenson's crazy matchmaking ideas. "We really need to get going. It was nice seeing you again." She turned and called for Rebecca. She placed the items from her cart on the counter and whipped out her credit card.

Safe inside the car, Melanie closed her eyes. A picture of Jackson at Aunt Phoebe's front door, holding calla lilies, flashed in her mind. Her eyes flew open, and she reached for her water. She guzzled the last drop and wished she had more. She peeked over to the rearview mirror. "Are you all buckled in?"

Rebecca nodded, still snuggling the bag of marshmallows. "Miss Melanie, do you think you and my daddy will ever go on a real date?"

Breathless, she was struggling for the right answer when her cell phone chirped. She glanced at the screen and turned around. "I'm sorry, sweetie. It's my office calling. I'm working on an important case." She leaned back into the seat. Although she had already spent numerous hours on the phone and via email working on this kidnapping case, Melanie was relieved she could avoid the question she wished deep down she could have answered with a yes.

* * *

With the last of the furniture loaded onto the truck, Jackson headed to The Bean. Wearing a wide grin, he was anxious to see Rebecca and hear all about her afternoon. The idea of Rebecca and Melanie baking together, something so common for mothers and daughters, warmed his heart. He yearned for Rebecca to have these experiences, but he was hesitant to want them with someone who wouldn't be around for the long term.

Jackson hopped into his truck and headed down the gravel driveway. He decelerated when a family of deer passed and disappeared into the woods. A red-tailed hawk circled above the driveway in search of its prey. Jackson loved Phoebe's property. It was always so full of life.

Ten minutes later, Jackson arrived at The Bean. He decided to sneak a peek through the window. He loved to watch Rebecca play when she didn't realize he was around. He smiled at the memory of her standing in front of her mirror with her pillowcase draped over her head, pretending it was a wedding veil. With no idea he was watching, she said her vows to Louis, her favorite teddy bear.

Jackson tiptoed around to the side window, which allowed for a better view of the entire kitchen. He cupped his hands to his brow and leaned forward. With no sun on this side of the restaurant, the glass was cold. His heart melted when he spied Rebecca wearing a red apron with white hearts. She stood on the step stool and snatched a pinch of cookie dough from the mixing bowl as Melanie stirred.

Melanie stole his breath. Her dark, wavy hair was pulled back into a ponytail, and a few pieces escaped the band. She wore the same apron as Rebecca.

As he continued to watch, thoughts invaded his head. He imagined the three of them as a family, taking trips to the beach and having Saturday-morning pancakes together.

What was he thinking? Melanie was here for one reason only.

When he heard laughter, he took one last look. They were taking turns dotting flour on each other's face. A stranger would assume they were mother and daughter.

He headed toward the front door, his pace slower. The wide grin he'd worn earlier was no longer present as he turned the doorknob and the bell jingled. "Hello—anyone home?"

Rebecca ran from the kitchen like a greyhound making its first lap around the track. "Daddy, you're here!" She flew into his arms and hugged him as though she'd never let go. He wished she wouldn't.

"It looks like someone's having fun." He put her down, but he could tell she was still flying on cloud nine after her afternoon of baking.

Melanie came through the kitchen door smiling, and Rebecca ran toward her. She grabbed Melanie's hand and led her toward Jackson. "Look at our aprons, Daddy. We're twins."

Despite their difference in hair color, they did look like twins. Right down to the dots of flour still on their faces. "So I see. I don't remember that apron, Rebecca." He glanced at Melanie, who was busy brushing the flour off her cheeks.

"Miss Melanie bought them at the market today. Don't you just love the little hearts?" A smile crept across her face and she performed a couple of rapid twirls. She giggled and raced back into the kitchen. "I'm going to wash the dishes. I love to play with the bubbles."

Jackson turned to Melanie, and they both shared a laugh. "I haven't seen Rebecca this happy in a long time."

Melanie shook her head. "That's silly, Jackson. Rebecca is one of the happiest little girls I've ever met."

It was true—she was a happy child—but he'd witnessed times when she was with her friends and their mothers and she looked so sad. Since Melanie's arrival, he hadn't seen the look. Now she had a light ignited from within, one he'd never seen before. "She's different, Mel, and I think you know why." He looked down at the floor, his face warm.

Melanie played with the chain around her neck and bit her lip. "We're just having fun baking. It's nothing, really."

He looked up at her response. "It is something, Mel. You're introducing her to a world she's never known." Jackson placed his hand under Melanie's chin and turned her face to the side. His legs grew weak when he leaned in and gently kissed her cheek. He pulled away when her body jerked. Their eyes locked, and he dropped his hand when she stepped back.

She examined his face. "I'm not sure what you mean, Jackson."

"Don't you see? You're showing her what it's like to have a mother."

She threw her hand across her mouth. "I'm sorry. It wasn't my intention. I only wanted to help you. We're just having fun."

He'd gone too far. He should have kept his thoughts to himself. Kissing her—what was he thinking? He reached his hand to hers, but she didn't accept it. "No, I'm sorry. You don't have to apologize. But obviously mothering comes natural to you. You're glowing."

The glow disappeared when she shook her

head. "It used to come natural, Jackson, but not anymore."

"That's not true. I've seen it with my own eyes. I've heard it in the sound of Rebecca's laughter. You have to believe it, Mel."

She walked toward the counter and slid into a stool. Emotion gleamed deep in her eyes. "I'm not sure what to believe anymore. What I do know is you're concerned about Rebecca becoming too attached. When I go back to DC, you're afraid she'll feel abandoned."

He agreed.

"Believe me, I get it. I know your job is to protect your daughter from pain. I have a tremendous amount of respect for you for feeling that way." She looked down at her fingers and twisted the only ring she wore. It looked like a wedding ring, but she wore it on her middle finger. "The last thing in the world I'd ever want to do is hurt your precious little girl." She paused when her voice began to shake. "You have no idea how much she's changed me, Jackson. In just the few days I've been here, I've become a different person. The old Melanie is returning."

Jackson had seen a change. He wanted to ask her to stay, but what if she said no? His heart broke for her and whatever pain she carried from her past. "I think you and Rebecca are helping each other."

She cleared her throat, picked up the pitcher and poured herself a glass of water. She took two long drinks and placed the glass back into the puddle of condensation on top of the counter. "I haven't shared much about myself with you, Jackson. I apologize. Aunt Phoebe has honored my wishes not to share my past with you or anyone in the town. Perhaps in time I'll be able to open up to you."

Frustrated by the situation, Jackson sighed. "That's the thing, Mel. We don't have time." For the first time in so long, he wanted to spend time with a woman. Mel. He wanted to get to know her a little each day, but it was impossible.

"Because you think I'm going to pack up Aunt Phoebe and run back to DC." She rubbed the back of her neck and drew in a breath. "That's what you mean, right?"

"Of course it's what I mean. You came to the valley with a plan, and you strike me as the type of woman who always follows a plan to its finish."

"But sometimes plans change."

He blinked several times. "What do you mean?"

Melanie's chin rose. "I mean, I've told Richard that I'm not planning to sell Aunt Phoebe's house. I told her I was wrong to try to uproot her life here in Sweet Gum." A tear sneaked from her lashes. "I'm sorry for any pain I caused you. I'll be returning to DC alone, and I'm okay with that."

Was she? He had his doubts. "You've made the right decision about Phoebe, but are you sure you're alright?"

He hoped she'd say no. That the only way she'd be alright was if she also stayed, but his hope didn't last long.

She expelled a wavering sigh. "I'll be fine."

His breathing slowed. He turned and headed toward the kitchen. "I better check with Rebecca and make sure she hasn't flooded the place." He gave a half smile and left Melanie alone with her thoughts.

After investigating the kitchen thoroughly and snatching a snickerdoodle, Jackson realized Rebecca was quite content to continue to play in the bubbles. "Don't overdo it with the soap, munchkin."

She giggled and turned with bubbles up to her elbows. "I won't, Daddy. You go and talk to Miss Melanie. I'm fine."

He wasn't sure, but he thought his five-year-old was making an attempt at playing matchmaker. He smiled at the thought.

Jackson slipped into the dining area, but Melanie wasn't sitting at the counter. He spied her standing by the window, looking down at something in her hands. He continued to watch. She wiped her eyes several times. Whatever she held in her hands was obviously causing her pain.

He didn't want to startle her, so he approached with caution. "Melanie, are you okay?"

She jumped as though he'd placed a hot poker against her arm. Melanie crammed what looked like a photograph into her pocket.

"Jackson! You scared me. Why are you sneaking up on me?" she yelled loud enough that Rebecca ran from the kitchen, but stopped outside the door.

It took him a moment to gather his thoughts. "I wasn't sneaking up on you. I saw you from across the room, and you looked upset." He tilted his head and placed his hand on her arm. "I was trying not to scare you."

She turned with a jerk. "Well, you did."

Jackson watched while Melanie took notice of Rebecca in the room. She stood across the room, her eyes wide.

With her head down, Melanie strolled toward Rebecca. She cupped her chin and tipped her head up. "I'm sorry I raised my voice."

"You're not mad at Daddy, are you?" Her lower lip quivered.

"Of course not. He accidentally scared me, that's all."

Rebecca turned quickly toward Jackson.

He nodded. "Everything's fine, Rebecca."

"Okay, I'll go and finish the dishes. Are we going to see Sam soon?" Rebecca asked, wearing a smile like nothing had happened.

Jackson eyed Melanie. He wondered if she still wanted to go with them. Relief washed over him when she nodded a yes. "Go ahead and finish up the dishes, and then we'll leave," he said. His cell phone chirped. "Don't forget to put the cookies in the freezer for Monday."

"Okay." She skipped into the kitchen.

When Jackson's phone chirped a second time, without looking at the screen, he answered the call. "This is Jackson."

Like other times, silence filled the line. He ended the call and looked at the caller ID. Another unknown number. Yesterday, when he scanned through the calls, a few had come in at two and three in the morning. Who would call at that hour? He might never know.

Melanie narrowed her eyes. "Was it another hang-up?"

"Yes, and this is about the third or fourth call today." He tilted his head and crammed the phone into his pocket. "If this keeps up, I'll have to get my phone number changed."

"It might be a good idea." She paused and tugged at the bottom of her sweater. "About what just happened—I know you didn't mean to startle me, so let's forget about it."

He nodded.

Melanie rested her hand on his arm. "As for how I reacted when you kissed me, let me explain…"

The pain in her eyes pierced Jackson's heart. He knew she wasn't ready to talk…not yet. "It's okay, Mel. We don't have to talk about it right now."

He'd be patient and hope she'd come to realize Sweet Gum was where she belonged. But what if she didn't? Time was running out. He'd have to make his true feelings known—but could he?

Chapter Eleven

It was a typical Saturday morning. The Bean bustled with people. Chatter filled the restaurant, along with the sounds of sizzling bacon coming from the kitchen. A warmth filled Melanie's heart while she took in her surroundings. People were actually talking to one another from their seats across the room. This was something she'd never seen in DC. People there didn't even speak to the person they were dining with. Usually they had their faces buried in their phones. Upon inspection, Melanie didn't see one cell in sight. She was in a different world. Was it one she could belong to?

"What's going on in that head of yours?" Jackson approached her with a plate of scrambled eggs, two bacon pieces and two slices of wheat toast. "Here, you need to eat, because I know you probably had only coffee for breakfast this morning."

The instant she caught a whiff of the cooked meat, her stomach grumbled. He was right—she hadn't taken the time to eat this morning, and now she was starving. "How did you know I had only coffee? What if I said I made a huge breakfast of French toast and crispy fried bacon?" She arched her brow and smiled.

"I'd say you've got a pretty good imagination." He handed her the plate. "Here, why don't you go sit with Rebecca? I just about have her meal ready." Jackson pointed to the table in the far corner of the restaurant, next to the window.

Melanie smiled and took the plate. "You're right—I'm ravenous. The three cups of coffee are burning a hole in my empty stomach." She turned and moved across the dining-room floor.

At the table, the sun beamed through the window onto the child's golden hair. Unaware of Melanie's presence, Rebecca had her nose buried in a picture book. Melanie watched while her tiny lips moved through the words on the page. Her little finger was in constant motion, twisting a stray curl. Melanie recalled her girls. They had always been oblivious to their surroundings when reading, just like Rebecca.

She cleared her throat. "Do you mind if I join you?" Melanie waited with her plate in hand before taking a seat. Behind her, Jackson stood with Rebecca's breakfast. He placed it in front of her, winked and walked away.

A huge grin moved across Rebecca's face. "Miss Melanie, I didn't see you standing there."

Melanie placed her breakfast on the table, anxious to take the first bite. "That must be a good book. You were off in another world." She speared the scrambled eggs with her fork and took her first bite. They were seasoned with just the right amount of pepper and a little shredded and melted cheddar cheese on top. Jackson definitely knew how she liked her eggs. "What's the story about?"

Rebecca placed her *Dora the Explorer* bookmark inside her book and closed it. "Well, it's about a little boy, and he really wants a puppy. He goes to sleep one night and has a dream he lives on a puppy farm." She fingered the corner of the book.

"That's quite a dream," Melanie said and took a bite of her toast.

"Do you think that can happen, Miss Melanie?"

"What?" She placed her fork on the plate and leaned in toward Rebecca.

"That if we really want something, we'll dream about it?"

Many times, Melanie had dreams that her

family was back with her, but that didn't happen. She swallowed the lump in her throat. "I suppose it could."

"Do you want to know something?"

"Sure." Melanie's pulse increased.

Rebecca's blue eyes studied Melanie. She placed her hands under her chin and rested her elbows on the table. "Last night, I had a dream that you were my mommy."

Melanie's breakfast turned over in her stomach. She reached across the table for Rebecca's hand. Inside her own, the warmth from this tiny hand was powerful. Melanie longed to stay like this forever. A tear escaped. "That's the nicest thing anyone has ever said to me." She wiped her eyes, but several more tears fell.

"I'm sorry, Miss Melanie. I didn't mean to make you cry." Rebecca bit down on her lip.

"Oh no, these are happy tears." Melanie straightened her shoulders and leaned back in her chair. She smiled because they really were tears of joy. The past year, any thoughts of being a mother again had brought on a tidal wave of sadness. Now, sitting with this precious child, she didn't feel the need to hide her past any longer.

"I'm glad they're happy tears." Rebecca tilted her head and smiled.

A powerful urge to share a piece of her past

with Rebecca surged through her heart. At the tiny corner table, for the first time, Melanie spoke about her beautiful family who'd gone to heaven.

Jackson froze in his chair. Engrossed in telling her story, Melanie didn't notice that he'd sat at a nearby table to tackle some paperwork, and that he could hear every word. His pencil rested on the ledger book. He didn't intend to eavesdrop, but it was the only open table. As he listened to Melanie telling stories about her family, his heart ached for her and all she'd lost. He closed his eyes and pressed his fingers to his temples. *Lord, please watch over Melanie. She won't admit it, but she needs You.*

When Phoebe mentioned Melanie's difficult past, he assumed it was a nasty divorce. He never imagined such a tragedy. *How does someone survive such a loss? Especially someone who doesn't lean on God for strength?* He rubbed his eyes. He began to understand why she'd wanted to move Phoebe. Without her aunt, Melanie was alone in the world.

"Well, hello there, Jackson Daughtry."

The sound of Sara's voice rattled him from his thoughts. With both hands on her hips, dressed in blue jeans, a red flannel shirt and a cowboy hat, Sara was obviously enjoying her day off from the hospital.

She pulled a chair close to him and plopped down, not waiting for him to extend the offer. "Don't you ever take time off for some fun, Jackson?"

Jackson's head dropped when he saw Melanie turn around at the sound of Sara's voice. She appeared surprised to see him at a table so close to her and Rebecca. When she crossed her arms and eyed him, he wondered if maybe she was a little jealous Sara was paying him so much attention. He had to make it clear to Melanie that he had no interest in the nurse. His interest lay with a beautiful woman from DC. He turned to Sara. "Actually, I have had some fun recently."

Sara's eyebrow arched. "Really?" She glanced toward Melanie, who now wore a smile.

"Yes. Melanie and I went on a hike, and we had a picnic by the river." He leaned back in his chair, released a sigh and smiled. "It was the perfect fall day." Jackson looked at Melanie and gave her a wink.

"Oh…that sounds nice." She stood up and ran her hands down the front of her faded jeans. "Well, I'd better let you get back to work, then." She threw a pinched expression toward Melanie, grabbed her purse and was out the door.

Rebecca sprang to her feet and jumped over

to his table. "Daddy, can we all take Sam to the apple orchard this afternoon?"

Melanie slid into the chair next to Jackson. His heart pounded when he caught a whiff of vanilla. He didn't know if it was her shampoo or her perfume, but the sweet scent made him dizzy.

"Please, can we?" Rebecca repeated.

"Yeah…please, Jackson. I think it might be good for us to get out for some fresh air," Melanie pleaded with her eyes locked on his.

Would another visit to the orchard put the sparkle back into her eyes? Jackson picked his daughter up and placed her on his lap. "Miss Melanie was just at the orchard the other day." He hoped she wanted to go. He'd love to spend every waking hour with this woman. His pulse raced thinking about it.

"Daddy, it was Miss Melanie's idea." She turned to Melanie for backup.

Melanie was busy shredding a paper napkin when she looked up at Jackson. "That's right. I thought it would be fun to take Sam out there. Let him run around a bit."

His grin widened, and he pulled his cell out. "Let me call Larry and make sure it's okay for us to pick up Sam." He stood and placed Rebecca in the chair next to Melanie. "We'll head out after closing."

Jackson stepped outside. The sun was so bright he couldn't see the screen on his phone. He strolled under a Douglas fir, and after a few minutes talking to Larry, they were all set to pick up Sam.

And an hour later, The Bean was cleaned up for the weekend, and two adults, one child and a rambunctious puppy were headed to the orchard. They made a quick stop at the store for Rebecca's favorite meal of fried chicken, macaroni and cheese and biscuits. Of course, Aunt Phoebe's brownies were already stowed in the basket, slowly defrosting.

Jackson smiled, thinking he could get used to this outdoor dining, especially with Melanie coming along. His arm rested on the opened car window. The sky was clear and the air warm for October. The slight breeze carried the sweet smell of apples. He pulled the truck into the first empty spot.

"Can we ride the wagon, Daddy?" Rebecca yelled the moment she spied the carriage they used for the hayrides.

"I don't think they're offering rides today. We'll have to wait for the apple festival. It will be here before you know it." He hopped from the truck, and Melanie waited until he came around to open her door. He liked that. He took her hand and helped her from the vehicle. Jackson wore a silly grin, and their eyes remained glued on each other.

Rebecca giggled from the backseat. "Daddy, you're making goo-goo eyes at Miss Melanie." She grabbed Louis, her teddy bear, and buried her face to stifle the laughter.

Jackson and Melanie broke out laughing.

"I was not." He examined Melanie more closely. "Was I?" He winked and slammed the passenger door shut. Once Rebecca was out of the truck with Sam in her arms, they headed off to Melanie's favorite spot by the river.

"Rebecca, why don't you put Sam on the leash? It might do him good to get some exercise."

"Okay, but can Miss Melanie come with us to the apple festival?"

"Well, that's up to Miss Melanie."

Rebecca jumped up and down. Sam's head bobbled. "Please, will you come with us?"

"Yes, please." He plucked a brilliant red wildflower and handed it to Melanie.

She brought it to her nose. "Ah…it smells so good. Thank you." Melanie glanced at Rebecca. "I'd love to go with you."

With Sam on the leash, Rebecca skipped down the dirt path. She could hardly keep up with the dog. "Stay close, Rebecca," Jackson called out while he watched her arm being nearly pulled from its socket.

"There's nothing cuter than a child and a puppy together." Melanie smelled the flower again as she gazed at Rebecca and Sam.

Jackson took a deep breath. "I think there's nothing more beautiful than you holding that wildflower."

He saw the color bloom on her cheeks.

He cleared his throat. "Listen, about today at The Bean. I hope you didn't think I was eavesdropping on you and Rebecca." He hesitated and watched for her reaction, but there wasn't one. "I had some paperwork to do, and it was the only empty table."

Up ahead, Rebecca stopped in the clearing while Sam investigated a scent behind an oak tree.

Melanie stopped and turned to Jackson. She reached for his hand. "I'm glad you overheard us talking. I should have shared my past with you. I'm sorry for not trusting you sooner."

He knew all about trust issues, so he understood. But that was no longer the case with Melanie. She was getting into his heart. With the sun reflecting off her chestnut hair, he couldn't take his eyes off of her. After all she'd been through, she was apologizing to him. Jackson couldn't resist the urge any longer. He opened his arms and pulled her close to him, never wanting to let go. "You don't have to apologize for anything, Mel."

Chapter Twelve

Melanie let Jackson take the lead. He headed toward the river and spread out the blanket. So much had changed since she and Jackson had sat at this very spot. A tremendous weight was gone now that he knew she wasn't moving Aunt Phoebe, but more important, there were no more secrets about her past.

With Rebecca and Sam occupied, now was as good a time as any to field questions from Jackson. Melanie took a seat next to him, their elbows touching. "Jackson, I want you to know everything that happened last year." She took a deep breath and released it. "I'll answer any questions you have. I'm sure, with all the noise in The Bean, you probably heard only bits and pieces."

He reached over and held her hand. "Why

don't you tell me in your own way? But first, I want you to know how sorry I am for your loss."

Melanie turned at the sound of a whip-poor-will bird from a nearby gum tree. "The past year has been a blur. Some days it feels like it just happened, and other days, it's like an eternity ago." She paused to wipe a tear she could no longer hold back. "It was my fault, Jackson."

"What are you talking about? It was an accident." With his index finger, he rubbed her hand in a circular motion.

She pulled it out of his grasp and ran her fingers through her hair. "I should have been with my family. If I had, I would have been the one driving, not Jeff. He was a doctor and had just come off a twenty-four-hour shift." The ground beneath her started to spin. She gripped the blanket in preparation for another panic attack.

Jackson's eyes widened. "Mel, are you okay?"

She took in short consecutive breaths until the spinning stopped. "Sorry... I have these spells sometimes."

"Panic attacks?" He tilted his head.

She nodded and hoped Jackson didn't notice the heat that filled her face. "That's what the doctors say." It was difficult to admit this weakness. She'd always thought people who experienced them were unable to cope. Now she was one of those people.

"Don't be ashamed, Mel. It's very common in cases like yours. Please don't feel embarrassed."

Melanie pushed her hair away from her face. "I'm getting better at keeping the attacks under control." She smiled. "You would have liked him, Jackson…my husband. He was a lot like you."

Jackson smiled. "How so?"

She turned to answer. "He was a wonderful father. The twins were crazy about him. Unlike me, he didn't put work first." Her hand gripped her pant leg. "Family was the most important thing to him."

Jackson gave her hand a squeeze. "Listen, I think you're being too hard on yourself. The accident wasn't your fault. It's obvious from the way you talk about your family that you loved them more than anything. You have a demanding job. It sometimes must take priority."

Melanie spotted Rebecca pick up Sam and head toward the blanket. It was time to end this conversation and rein in her emotions. "Work should never be a priority over family. I know now. I only wish I'd realized then."

Rebecca jumped in the middle of the blanket and put the dog next to Jackson. "Daddy, we're hungry."

Melanie pulled Rebecca into her arms. Everything was right in the world when she was around. "You know, Rebecca, I didn't get to thank you for listening to me talk about my girls this morning."

Rebecca scrunched her forehead. "You don't have to thank me, Miss Melanie. I'm glad you were a mommy, even if it wasn't for a long time." She tapped her tennis shoes against the blanket.

She kissed Rebecca on the cheek. "How would you like a big piece of fried chicken?" Melanie gave her button nose a quick tap.

A half hour passed as they ate their picnic and enjoyed the view. "That was nearly as good as Phoebe's chicken." Jackson rested his hand across his stomach. "I'm so stuffed, I couldn't eat another bite."

"So, I guess I can have your brownie, then?" Melanie snatched the dessert and brought it to her lips, pretending to take a bite.

He grabbed it from her hand and placed it back inside the basket. "Not on your life."

Rebecca giggled.

When Jackson's cell phone chirped, he frowned. He answered and quickly hung up. "That's enough." He tossed the phone to the side.

"Was it another hang-up?" Melanie's eyebrows drew together. "I thought when I adjusted your settings it would take care of the problem with unknown calls. Do you want me to take another look?"

He shook his head. "I don't think it would do any good, but thanks for the offer." Jackson rubbed his hand across his chin. "I think whoever this is knows what they're doing when it comes to making sure their numbers don't show up. What I don't understand is why they call so often and never say a thing."

When his phone chirped a second time, Melanie picked it up off the blanket. A quick scan of the screen and she knew this call was safe. She handed it to Jackson. "It's Aunt Phoebe."

While he took the call, Melanie reached over to Sam and placed the puppy on her lap. "I've been meaning to ask—when do you get to take him home?" she asked, stroking the puppy's neck.

Rebecca flung herself back on the blanket and released a heavy sigh. "Oh… I don't know. It seems like it's been forever. Mr. Whiteside said he still needs his mommy."

She remembered how slowly time passed when she was a child. Once her girls were born, the time seemed to pass faster each year. "Be patient. You'll be bringing Sam home before you know it."

Jackson said goodbye and turned to Melanie. "Uh…just so you know, I didn't mention us being together to Phoebe. I wasn't sure if it was something you wanted to share with her yourself."

"I appreciate it, Jackson. What was she calling about?"

"She wants me to pick her up and take her to church tomorrow. Apparently the doctor said it was okay since she's doing so well."

Melanie's shoulders wilted. "I planned on visiting her tomorrow."

Jackson wiped his hands down the front of his jeans. "Well, she asked me if I'd bring you to church, too."

Melanie squirmed on the blanket. Even though she'd been able to open up to Jackson about the accident, there was no way she was ready to attend church.

"Yes, please, Miss Melanie, come to church with us. Maybe after, we can all go out for Sunday dinner." Rebecca was on her feet, twirling on the blanket. Sam nipped at her heels.

Melanie's heart sank. Rebecca had helped her so much. How could she possibly say no? Then there was Aunt Phoebe. She'd be disappointed, as well. "Okay, I'll go, but only if we can have another picnic here afterward." There was something about this place. This spot in particular brought Melanie a sense of peace.

Her wish was to spend as much time here as possible before going back to DC.

"Three picnics?" Jackson winked at Melanie. "I believe this mountain air is growing on you."

"I think you might be right."

Rebecca grabbed a brownie. "Daddy, can I take Sam for a walk? I'm tired of sitting, and he's getting bored."

"Okay, but don't go too far, and please stay in sight." Jackson opened the picnic basket, grabbed two brownies and handed one to Melanie. "I think I'm hungry again." He grinned. "These are a little different from the others."

Melanie snatched the offering. It looked more like two stacked on top of each other with something gooey in the center. She took a huge bite. "Yum… This just melts in your mouth." She took another bite. "Is that peanut butter?" She licked the chocolate that oozed between her fingers.

Jackson laughed and reached for her hand. "Don't bite off a finger, now."

His touch triggered a shiver that traveled up her spine. This felt right. Could this be a new beginning for her? "Jackson, can I ask you something?"

"Of course—anything."

Since Rebecca had brought up her mother during dinner at Aunt Phoebe's house, Melanie had been curious about her. "Has Rebecca's mother ever tried to get in contact with her?"

He shook his head. "No. She left when Rebecca was a year old, and I've never heard from her since." Jackson glanced up to the sky. "Funny thing, she ran off with one of my best friends from high school." He shrugged his shoulders. "I never heard from him again, either."

Melanie picked at her fingernail. Why had she even brought up the subject? It was obviously painful for Jackson, but she wanted to know more. "It must have been so hard."

"The hardest part was losing the trust of two people who I loved, and who I thought loved me." He let out a faint breath.

She studied his chiseled features. As she recalled the feeling of his lips against her cheek, she wondered how they would feel against her lips. As though he read her mind, Jackson leaned in closer. The warmth of his breath on her face tickled. When he pulled back ever so slightly, she leaned forward. This feeling, this moment—she wanted it to last forever.

"Daddy, daddy…come quick!"

At the sound of his daughter's call for help, Jackson shot up like a rocket and took off running. Melanie's foot twisted in the blanket when she tried to get up.

After several jerks, her foot finally free, she sprinted toward Rebecca's cries. The sound of the water racing filled her mind with terrible thoughts. Had she fallen into the river?

Melanie's breath caught in her throat at the sight of the little girl's blond curls. Standing next to the rushing water with her hands covering her eyes, she screamed, "Sam fell into the river."

Jackson snatched his daughter into his arms and held her tight. "Tell us exactly what happened." With a gentle hand, he rubbed her back in a circular motion.

"Sam saw a rabbit and took off running." She released a piercing wail. "The leash burned my hand. I couldn't hold on. I killed him."

Jackson passed Rebecca into Melanie's arms. "I'll find him." He turned and sprinted down the path.

"How do you know he fell into the river?" Melanie scanned the area. "Maybe he chased a bunny along the bank."

Rebecca's eyes were bloodred. Her tears continued to flow, soaking Melanie's shirt. "I'm scared. He's so little." Her lips trembled uncontrollably. "I shouldn't have taken him from his mommy this soon. It's my fault."

Melanie's stomach lurched. *It's my fault.* She knew all too well what Rebecca was feeling. She lived with it every day. She was the twins' mother. It was her job to protect them. Her own tears coursed down her cheeks.

"Miss Melanie?" Rebecca's tears slowed, and her tiny hand touched Melanie's face. "Why are you crying? Are you sad about Sam, too?"

Melanie hugged the precious child, no longer feeling the fear of being close to her. She longed for her own girls back in her arms, but that would never happen. "It's not your fault, sweetie. Sometimes things happen we can't control."

"Like the accident?"

Rebecca's words splintered Melanie's heart. She wanted to rip the pain from her chest. She gulped. "You mean my accident? When your daddy rescued me?"

"No, the accident that sent your family to heaven. You couldn't control it…could you?"

The words lodged deep in her throat. Melanie could only shake her head.

"Daddy says God is in control. He knows what's best for us."

Melanie wiped her eyes, craving more. "Really… What else does your daddy say?"

"He says sometimes bad things happen we don't understand, but God knows." A closed-lip smile took over her face. "He'll make it all good in the end." With a gentle touch, she brushed a loose strand of hair away from Melanie's eyes.

Melanie paused to consider Jackson's words, passed on to her by his beautiful child. Was God trying to make good in the end? Had He brought Rebecca and Jackson into her life for a purpose? Her mind raced. Was He trying to fulfill her dream of having another family? A dream she believed was impossible to capture, given her career-driven life in DC?

Rebecca's head jerked and she pointed down the path. "Look, Miss Melanie! Daddy is coming, and he has Sam."

Rebecca squirmed in her arms, but Melanie didn't want to let go. Ever.

"See, Miss Melanie, my daddy is pretty smart."

Melanie's heart lifted at the sight of Jackson walking toward them and holding the puppy. She laughed, watching it smother Jackson's face with wet licks. She turned and looked at Rebecca. This was what a family felt like. "Yes, he sure is."

Jackson couldn't recall the last time he'd been this content. Sitting in the church pew with his daughter on one side and Melanie on the other, he thought his heart might explode with joy.

He leaned down when Rebecca turned to him and cupped her hand as if to whisper a secret in his ear. "We're like a family, Daddy." Her eyes

were alight with fire. He reached for her hand
and gave it a squeeze.

Something in Melanie had changed yesterday, and Jackson couldn't have been happier.
The hurt once consuming her eyes was now replaced with a sparkle. Jackson didn't ever want
to look away.

Phoebe, of course, had noticed immediately.
When they'd picked her up for church, all it
took was one look. "You're positively glowing.
Working at The Bean must agree with you,"
she'd told Melanie.

Watching Mel today in church, Jackson
agreed. She was more beautiful than ever, if it
were even possible.

When the service concluded, the congrega-
tion filed out. The pastor greeted everyone with
a handshake. "It's good to see you, Jackson." He
glanced at Melanie and gave Jackson a wink.
"I'm so happy you decided to join us, Melanie.
I hope we'll see you again."

Melanie blushed. "I hope so, too, Pastor. It
was a lovely service."

Outside, Rebecca grabbed Jackson's hand.
"Daddy, can Miss Melanie take me over to the
playground for a few minutes?" His daughter's
eyes pleaded for more time with her.

Jackson glanced toward Melanie, who nodded.

Phoebe stepped forward. "It sounds like a

wonderful idea." She ruffled the top of Rebecca's curls. "I need to speak with your daddy in private."

He took notice of the raised eyebrow Melanie gave Phoebe. "Okay," he said, "but only for a few minutes if you want to go on the picnic." He'd woken up extra early this morning to make ham-and-Swiss-cheese sandwiches on rye bread and potato salad. He'd also defrosted more of the fudge brownies since Melanie was crazy about them. With everything stowed in the cooler inside his truck, they were ready.

"Okay, Daddy." Rebecca grabbed Melanie's hand, and they took off running toward the playground. Melanie's flowered dress blew in the breeze. It was a good thing she was wearing flats.

"Jackson, what on earth has become of my Melanie?" The older lady beamed. "She's so happy. I haven't seen her this way since she lost her family."

Jackson kicked a few pebbles, stirring up a little dust. "Yesterday at the orchard, she told me about her family and the accident." He paused. "I don't think I've ever met a woman as strong as her. What she experienced... I just don't know if I could move on."

Her gazed flicked to Melanie and Rebecca, who were across the grounds. "It's been a difficult path for her, but I'm thankful she's finally opened up to you."

Relief washed over him, but he wasn't quite sure how Phoebe would feel about the two of them getting close. "I think Rebecca has really helped Mel to open up."

"Mel?" She crossed her arms and flashed a smile.

He stuffed his hands in the front pockets of his slacks. "It's just a little nickname." He grinned, and warmth moved across his face.

"I think if the truth be told, you've really helped Melanie. I see the way she looks at you, Jackson." Tears peppered Phoebe's eyelashes. "Thank you for bringing my niece back to me."

The past few days, Jackson had assumed Rebecca was responsible for the transformation in Melanie. He'd never imagined he could have contributed. "Well, I really haven't done anything other than help with The Bean."

Phoebe lifted an eyebrow. "She told me about the picnics, Jackson. Last night on the phone, she couldn't stop talking about it. Melanie sounded like a high-school girl with her first crush."

He felt like a teenager himself. Each day he was growing closer to Melanie, and to his surprise, he wasn't questioning his judgment in the trust department. This was a new and exciting feeling. One he hoped to explore.

"I'll be honest with you. Melanie is becoming an important person, not only in my life but also in Rebecca's." He paused and placed his hand on her arm. "I hope it's okay with you. I wouldn't want to do anything to jeopardize our relationship." Jackson leaned over and kissed her cheek. "You know, next to Rebecca, you're the most important woman in my life."

Phoebe grabbed his hand and gave it a firm squeeze. "I don't know, Jackson. It sounds as though Melanie's giving me a little competition, but it's quite alright with me."

Several hours later, with bellies full, they drove Phoebe back to the rehabilitation center.

Phoebe sat in the front seat with Jackson, while Melanie and Rebecca sat in the back listening to music. Rebecca had Jackson's iPod and a set of earbuds. Melanie wore one bud while Rebecca wore the other. Their heads bobbed to the music. They giggled and whispered to each other like best friends.

Phoebe leaned toward Jackson and spoke in a hushed tone. "They're like two peas in a pod. I simply can't get over the change in my niece."

Jackson nodded. "I'd prayed Melanie would change her mind about moving you to DC, and the good Lord answered."

"What do you think changed her mind?"

He'd been confident in her reason for the change. "At The Bean the other day, when the stove broke and so many people came by to help out, she commented on how many people cared about you."

Phoebe nodded and smiled. "This is where I belong."

He had to admit, Melanie had done a three-sixty since the first night when they'd had dinner at Phoebe's. Perhaps with more time, he could convince her to stay in Sweet Gum.

"I have a plan, but I'll need your help." She glanced over her shoulder and turned back toward Jackson. Her eyes shifted. She looked quite mischievous. It was nice to see Phoebe getting back to her old self.

"You know I'll help you any way I can."

"The doctor said I'm doing really well. In fact, he thinks I'll be able to return home and back to The Bean, but part-time only."

"That's great news. Why didn't you tell Melanie?" He gripped the steering wheel a little tighter when he came upon a herd of deer grazing off the side of the road.

"I plan to tell her I'm being released on Wednesday, but I'd rather she didn't know I've been cleared to return to The Bean."

Jackson glanced into his rearview mirror and

saw both passengers were still engrossed in the music. There was no way they could hear the secret conversation going on in the front seat. "Why wouldn't you want her to know?"

"Well, I don't plan to return to The Bean... at least not yet."

"Don't you want to go back? You love that place. It was your and my mother's dream." Jackson worked his jaw back and forth.

Phoebe folded her hands in her lap. "I do love it, but I love Melanie more."

Jackson raised a brow, unsure where Phoebe was going with this. "What does Melanie have to do with this decision?"

"I see the change in her. Spending time with you and Rebecca, working with you at The Bean, has been so good for her. I never thought you'd be able to convince her to come to church today." Phoebe paused and gazed out the window. "By the way, I see the way you look at her, too, Jackson."

He barely kept his smile in check at the thought of spending more time with Melanie. He had plenty of leave from his job and couldn't think of a better way to spend it than with the woman who'd stolen his heart. Still, he knew Phoebe, and he couldn't help but wonder if she was trying to play matchmaker. He smiled at the idea and secretly hoped she was.

Phoebe laughed. "The way you're smiling, you look like a lovesick schoolboy." She reached for his hand resting on the console. "She needs you, Jackson, and I think you need her, too."

From the backseat, with music blaring in one ear, Melanie couldn't hear what Jackson and Aunt Phoebe were talking about, but they were definitely engrossed in conversation. She couldn't stand it any longer. She ripped the earbud from her ear and leaned forward. "So, what are you two whispering about up there?"

Aunt Phoebe turned around. "We weren't whispering. You have the music up too loud." She winked at Jackson.

Since Jackson knew about the accident, Melanie didn't have to worry about her secret being revealed. Still, she was curious. "So come on—tell me."

Phoebe cleared her throat and laughed. "It's nothing earth-shattering. Dr. Roberts plans to release me from rehabilitation on Wednesday."

Melanie's shoulders straightened. "That's great news. Why didn't you say something earlier?" She reached over the seat and patted her shoulder.

"I found out only this morning. Besides, I was so excited to be outside of the rehab and enjoying the fresh air, I guess it slipped my mind."

A heavy weight settled into Melanie's chest. Although she was thrilled to hear Aunt Phoebe was getting better, this would mean Melanie wouldn't be needed at The Bean any longer. The time spent working with Jackson and Rebecca would end. There'd be no reason for her to stay, leaving her with no option but to return to DC. Her heart ached at the thought.

"Melanie, are you okay? You're a million miles away." Jackson eyed her in the rearview mirror.

The gentle touch of Rebecca's hand on her back was a reminder of what she would miss when she was gone. "Miss Melanie, does it mean you have to go back to DC?"

"Wait a minute, everyone. You didn't let me finish telling you Dr. Roberts's orders. He's releasing me from rehab, but I'll continue working with an at-home therapist. Most importantly, he said I wasn't ready to return to work full-time."

A glimmer of hope filled Melanie. Of course, she wanted Aunt Phoebe to recover and do all of the things that made her happy. Still, Melanie wasn't ready to lose her position at The Bean.

"Yippee! So we can all keep working together." Rebecca bounced up and down in the seat. Her curls sprang in all directions. Then, with a jerk, she stopped. "I'm sorry, Phoebe. It's not that I don't want you better… It's just, if you come back to The Bean, Miss Melanie will leave."

Melanie's cheeks infused with heat. *Leave.* Was DC where she belonged? After her time spent in Sweet Gum, she didn't know anymore.

Aunt Phoebe turned toward Rebecca. "It's okay. I know what you mean. I don't want Melanie to go, either."

Listening to them talk about her leaving made Melanie feel as though she had millipedes crawling on her skin. Could she build a new life here? What about her job? It was all she had, but what kind of life was it?

Jackson pulled into the parking lot of the rehabilitation center. "Well, it's settled. We'll continue to run things as we've been doing." He turned to Phoebe. "You take all the time you need. We've got it covered."

His words made her heart soar. She was giddy at the thought of continuing to work with Jackson. At this moment, her job in DC seemed a million miles away.

She unfastened her seat belt and gripped the door handle. "I'll take Phoebe inside." She opened the door and extended her hand to help her aunt out of the truck.

Inside, the smell of lavender filled the older woman's room. "You know, until I came here, I hadn't smelled lavender in years."

"You should come back in the spring, Melanie. The entire valley smells of it." She tilted the blinds to block the sun that beamed into her eyes.

Melanie remained silent.

"Dear, I know what you're thinking. You don't want to leave." She walked toward Melanie and reached for her hand. "That's where your mind was, wasn't it?"

She nodded.

"In the time you've been in the valley, I think you've come to love this place as much as I do. You've seen the people in this town, and how important they are to me. I think you're feeling the same way." She cupped Melanie's chin, and their eyes locked.

Standing in Aunt Phoebe's room with the bed neatly made and a flowered quilt perfectly folded, Melanie knew it was time to admit to herself that her heart now belonged to the valley.

Her lip quivered. "The thought of going back to DC alone terrifies me, but my firm needs me. They made national news after the kidnapping incident. If it weren't for me and the long hours I spent on the phone in negotiations, my client would have never gotten her son back."

"Why didn't you tell us? This is wonderful news—you should be proud."

Melanie pinned her arms against her stomach. At first she was excited to share the outcome, but then she felt guilty and self-absorbed. "I didn't feel right talking about my job with you, or Jackson."

Her aunt frowned. "But why?"

"It's the reason I no longer have a family. I don't know what to do. If I leave DC, I'll be abandoning the memories of my family." A sour taste crept into her throat.

"You'll never abandon those memories, dear." She placed her fingers on her niece's heart. "They'll always remain here, no matter where you go. Give it time, dear. God will give you the answer you're looking for. He knows exactly what's right for you and where you should be." She snatched a tissue from the box sitting on her dresser and dabbed Melanie's eyes.

"How will I know if it's right?" Melanie took another tissue and blew her nose.

"If God puts it in your heart, Melanie, trust me, you'll know."

Chapter Thirteen

Wednesday morning, Jackson was flying solo at The Bean. Melanie and Rebecca had gone to pick up Phoebe from the rehabilitation center.

The restaurant was slow, so he spent most of the morning mopping the kitchen floor and doing some paperwork.

The past two days, Jackson had been happier than he'd been in years. The attraction between him and Melanie was obviously growing. At first he'd thought it was one-sided, but he'd caught her staring a few times. A couple of times she'd acted a little flirty. He loved it. A weight was removed when she told him she didn't plan to take Phoebe back to DC. Now he was on a mission to keep Mel right here, where she belonged.

"Hey, Jackson." The shrill of Sara's voice stole his joyous thoughts.

He placed the mop inside the bucket and grabbed the dish towel to dry his hands. "I'll be out in a minute."

The kitchen door flew open, and in walked Sara, dressed in a short pink skirt, too short for this time of the year, and heels way too high for walking. "Are you here all by your little old self?" Her eyes skimmed the room then fixed back on him.

Jackson leaned against the counter and crossed his arms. "Yes, I am. What's up, Sara?"

She took a couple of steps toward him. "So, does this mean Melanie went back to DC? I didn't think someone like her would last too long in such a small town. She's probably used to rich men and fancy cars."

He shoved his hands in his pockets. If Sara was trying to raise doubt about a possible relationship with Melanie, she was doing a good job. Maybe Melanie couldn't be happy here. Her life was her job, and there was no need for a high-powered divorce attorney in Sweet Gum. After all, folks around here stayed married. "What do you want, Sara? I've got a lot of work to do."

She placed her hands on her hips and pursed her lips. "I picked up some steaks at the market this morning. I wondered if you'd like to come over for dinner." Her eyes burned through him.

"I'm sure you know your way around a grill better than me."

Jackson almost felt sorry for her, but he knew Sara too well, and he didn't want to lead her on. Besides, she'd just bounce along to another guy if she got a no from him. "Thanks for the invitation, but Melanie, Rebecca and I are cooking for Phoebe tonight. It's her first night back home from rehab."

Sara's eyebrow arched. "I thought Melanie went back to DC."

He chuckled. "I never said it. You did." Jackson took in a heavy breath. Now was the time to let Sara know they had no future. His future was with Melanie. At least, he prayed it would turn out that way. "Look, Sara, I don't want to come off as a jerk, but Melanie and I are kind of dating."

Sara's shoulders slumped while she slowly walked toward the door. When she turned, Jackson thought he saw a tear slide down her cheek. "I'm glad you're happy, Jackson. Really, I am. I only hope she doesn't break your heart. No one deserves that twice in a lifetime."

Alone in the kitchen, Jackson thought about what Sara had said. He had prayed Melanie would decide to stay, and now it was up to her, but he'd do his best to convince her. He was willing to risk a broken heart if it meant there was a chance they could both get their happily-ever-after.

Later in the evening, while Phoebe and Rebecca worked a jigsaw puzzle at Phoebe's dining-room table, Jackson found himself wrestling with a pot of spaghetti noodles.

"Jackson, what in the world are you doing?" Melanie turned, her hair swept up in a loose bun, highlighting her delicate features.

"Jackson!"

With a jerk, he turned from the stove. "Did you say something, Mel?"

She laughed. "What's wrong with you tonight?" She dropped the cucumber slices into the salad. "You seem so distracted."

This beautiful woman, who he wanted to spend every moment with, was his distraction. "I'm sorry. I'm just concentrating on the noodles."

"Yeah, noodles require a lot of attention." She rolled her eyes. "You're so funny."

His cell phone chirped. He dried his hands on the dishrag and yanked the phone from his pocket. The screen said the caller was unknown, but he answered anyway.

"This is Jackson."

This time there was definitely someone on the line. "Who is this?" The breathing carried through the phone line. "What do you want?"

Click.

He crammed the phone into his pocket and turned his attention back to Melanie. As annoying as the calls had been, there was no way he'd let them interfere with their alone time. With Phoebe's health improving, it was only a matter of time before Melanie would be gone, but the footprints she'd leave on his heart would remain.

Melanie knew these constant phone calls and hang-ups were upsetting Jackson. He didn't mention anything after the recent call, but his red face told her his patience was wearing thin. If he wanted to talk about it, she'd let him bring it up.

"Ouch!" With her thoughts on Jackson and not the sharp knife, she'd cut her hand and was now bleeding all over the onions.

Jackson raced to her side and grabbed her hand. "Mel, this is a serious cut." He took the knife from her hand and grabbed a clean dish towel from the drawer next to the sink.

"I don't think Aunt Phoebe will appreciate me getting blood all over her nice towels." She closed her eyes, hating the sight of blood, especially when it was her own.

"We've got to apply pressure to stop the bleeding. It doesn't look like you'll need stitches, but you cut yourself good."

She chewed her lip. "I wasn't paying attention, I guess." She was certainly paying attention to Jackson's warm breath tickling her neck like a summer ocean breeze.

"Let's give it a good rinse and see if the bleeding has stopped." He removed the towel and turned on the water. Their eyes met, and he held her gaze. "Let it run for a second to warm up."

Melanie needed water, but not on her hand. A jump into a cold swimming pool, in the middle of a snowstorm, was what she needed. Her temperature skyrocketed.

"It looks like the bleeding stopped," Jackson said. He turned off the warm water. "I'll just bandage it up and you'll be good to go."

As he continued to hold on to her hand, Melanie stared up into his eyes. "Look at you, coming to my rescue again, Jackson." She inched her head closer, feeling his breath, this time against her cheek.

He lowered his head, his cheeks red. "I guess I am."

When his lips brushed against hers, chills traveled through her body. His lips were tender, just as she'd imagined they'd be. Was she really kissing Jackson Daughtry? The floor dropped from under her, and the thrill was better than any Ferris wheel. Her lips moved with certainty, and her heart told her he was the one.

"Daddy, come look at our puzzle," Rebecca shouted from the dining room.

The Ferris wheel came to an abrupt halt at the sound of Rebecca's voice. Jackson jumped like a grasshopper dodging the lawn mower, and she steadied herself against the counter. They exchanged a grin.

In her sock feet, Rebecca skidded into the kitchen and grabbed his hand, pulling him toward the dining room.

"Hold on a minute. Miss Melanie cut her hand, and I need to bandage it for her."

Rebecca skipped toward Melanie and reached for her hand. She lightly brushed her lips against it. "Daddy always kisses my boo-boos to make them better." She turned on her heel and scampered out of the room.

Jackson turned to Melanie. "Well, I guess my aim was a little off with the kiss." He winked and pulled the first-aid kit from the pantry.

She lifted her gaze to his. "I don't know. I thought it was right on target." She grinned and extended her hand so he could wrap it.

"Before we get interrupted again, I wanted to ask you if you'd like to go out to dinner tomorrow night."

Melanie's heart raced. "Like a date?"

Jackson cut the piece of gauze and carefully applied a dollop of antibacterial ointment. Her skin tingled in response to his gentle touch. Wearing a gentle smile, he began to wrap her hand.

"Yes, just the two of us. I already checked with Phoebe. Of course, she's thrilled about the idea. She said she'd watch Rebecca."

Melanie blinked. Heat rose in her cheeks at the thought of one-on-one time with him. "That would be nice."

"I know just the place. You'll love it." He stuck on the last piece of tape to secure the bandage. "I'll pick you up at seven."

"I'll be ready."

The following morning, Melanie woke with a smile. She stared at the cedar ceiling, one of her favorite things about the room, and recalled the gentle kiss she and Jackson had shared.

The smell of freshly brewed coffee pulled Melanie from her memories. She slipped her feet into her favorite pink fuzzy slippers, grabbed her robe and headed toward the kitchen.

Sun streamed through the plantation shutters. She quickly spotted a fully dressed Aunt Phoebe at the stove, cooking something that smelled like onions and very delicious. Her stomach rumbled on cue.

"You're already dressed and ready for the day." Melanie glanced down at her flowered robe and slippers. "I think this mountain air is making me lazy."

Aunt Phoebe turned at the sound of her voice. "I think the valley is growing on you, along with a fella by the name of Jackson Daughtry." She turned her attention back to the stove and carefully poured the beaten eggs into the skillet.

"I haven't slept this late in years." She grabbed the coffeepot and a huge mug with a smiley face on the front and took a sip. "Ah...your coffee is always the best."

Aunt Phoebe laughed. "The mood you're in now, I could have used dirt and water to make the coffee and you wouldn't notice the difference. Let me guess. Jackson is the reason for that smile you've got plastered from ear to ear."

Melanie climbed onto the bar stool at the island and placed her cup on the granite countertop. "Yes—tonight is the big night. My stomach has butterflies, possibly bats. Do you know how long it's been since I've been on a date?"

"Relax and enjoy yourself. You and Jackson will have a wonderful time."

She ran her finger along the top of her coffee mug. Steam drifted from the top. "Can I ask you something?"

Phoebe turned the burner off and slipped onto the stool next to her. "You can ask me anything."

"Do you think it's too soon for me to get romantically involved? I mean, it's been only a year since the accident."

"Oh dear, is that what you're worried about?" She reached for Melanie's hand. "A year is a long time. Jeff would want you to be happy."

She wiped a tear with the sleeve of her robe. "Yes, he would. I'd want the same for him. It's just…it feels like I'm cheating on him."

Aunt Phoebe leaned in closer to Melanie. "Listen to me. You'll never find a better and more honest man than Jackson Daughtry. You're so young, you'd be cheating yourself if you didn't take a chance on love again. Besides, God has brought the two of you together for a reason."

Melanie wasn't sure if God had orchestrated this, but she did know Jackson was a good man. He and Rebecca brought joy back into her heart. Something she thought she'd never experience again. She reached over and took Aunt Phoebe into her arms. "If it weren't for you, I'd still be hiding from the world in DC. Thank you."

"Okay now, there's a cheese-and-onion omelet in the skillet, and it's got your name on it."

"It smells scrumptious." Melanie rubbed her empty stomach. "After I eat and shower, I've got to run some errands. Do you need anything while I'm out?"

"You're not going to The Bean today?"

"Nope." Melanie grinned. "My generous boss gave me the day off to go shopping for an outfit for tonight. I have an appointment at the quaint boutique in town. The one with the pink lace curtains in the window."

"Yes, Estelle's place. She's a wonderful and dear friend. Don't be late for your appointment. She's a busy lady." Aunt Phoebe tore a piece of paper from the notepad sitting on the corner of the island. "Here are a couple of things I need from the market." She passed her the list. "Oh, and can you take the box of menus and drop it off at The Bean?" She grabbed the spatula and put the omelet on the plate. "Before my stroke, I thought the current menus needed a little updating. The printing company had some technical difficulties, but they were finally delivered yesterday, and they look great."

Melanie glanced toward the box on the floor. "Sure, I'd be happy to." Thrilled she didn't have to wait until tonight, her heart fluttered at the thought of seeing Jackson this morning. She smiled, thinking of Rebecca's words: *It will be the best day ever.*

Chapter Fourteen

Jackson's morning wasn't going well. He'd burned a skillet of hash browns and dropped an entire bowl of pancake batter onto the kitchen floor. Despite the mishaps, as he mopped up the mess, he had a smile pasted on his face. He and Mel were going on their first date tonight. He hoped it would be the first of many, if he could convince her to stay.

The jingle of the bell alerted him to an incoming customer. He tossed the dish towel on the countertop and headed to the dining area.

"Hello, Jackson."

He froze, and a cold chill settled into his bones. When he rubbed his eyes, she was still there. Taylor, his ex-wife, stood in the middle of The Bean. Her once short, dark hair was now long and curly.

She rubbed her finger across her lip. "Aren't you going to say hello?"

"Taylor, what are you doing here?" He glanced around the dining area, thankful it was empty. More important, he was relieved Mary and her mother had picked Rebecca up earlier.

Taylor's high heels clicked a slow rhythm against the tile. She approached him with her arms open. Her leather pants swished. "Is that any way to welcome the mother of your child, Jackson?"

Alcohol. He smelled it when she moved in closer. "Why are you here?"

"Do you really think I would stay away? You know me better than that." She stumbled and reached for a nearby table.

Had she been the one calling? He'd had a suspicion that was the case. "Why all of the calls?"

Her eyes turned toward the floor. "I wanted to talk to you."

"So, why didn't you?"

"I was afraid—"

"Of what?"

Taylor studied him with glazed eyes. "I was scared you wouldn't want to talk to me." She paused. "I want us to get back together."

Jackson ran his hand across his face in disbelief. "You what?"

"Wilson and I are finished. I want to give our marriage another try."

She was talking crazy, and he'd heard enough. He wanted her gone. "I can tell you've been drinking, and I assume you were when you called obsessively. I need you to leave before any customers arrive."

"Are you worried about the customers or your little rich girlfriend?" She pursed her painted cherry Popsicle lips.

"Girlfriend?"

"Don't deny it, Jackson. I've seen you getting cozy with that woman." She stumbled again. "If you think she's going to take my place as Rebecca's mother, you're mistaken."

This was crazy. What was she doing here? Had she been following him? His face burned. "Mother? You call yourself a mother? You left your own daughter when she was only a year old. What kind of person does that?"

"I was messed up, Jackson." She dropped her purse on the ground. Its contents went flying.

"Oh, and now you're fine? I can smell the alcohol on your breath. It's ten in the morning, Taylor. You need to get some help. There's an excellent rehab program in Smithfield. I know the director. I could get you admitted."

"I'm sure you want nothing more than to lock me away for a few months. Then you and your little girlfriend can brainwash my daughter against me." She held up her arms. "There's no way I'm going into rehab." She glared.

He balled his hands into fists. "Fine. Let me call you a cab. You're in no condition to drive."

"I don't need one," she announced, stumbling on her heels.

"Then I'm going to call the police."

She staggered closer to Jackson and placed her finger on his chest. "I'm not leaving until I see my daughter."

Memories from the last time he'd seen her raced through his mind. The day she'd walked out with his best friend, Wilson. Four years later, she was no different. Her breath was foul and her eyes like red marbles. There was no way he'd let her anywhere near Rebecca.

"Please wait outside—I'll call the cab company," Jackson said. He turned to walk her toward the door.

Before he knew what was happening, she threw her arms around him and gave him a slobbering kiss.

"Get out of here, now!" Jackson pushed her away and she lost her footing, nearly falling onto the floor.

"I'm going to see my daughter if it's the last thing I do. You can't keep me from her."

Jackson watched, shaking his head. She

stumbled out the door, leaving her lipstick on the floor. As he walked to the kitchen to grab his phone, tires screeched outside. He grabbed the cell and tore to the front door. She was gone. His hands shook as he dialed the sheriff's office.

Melanie's heart was broken. When she'd seen Jackson kissing a tall brunette, she'd dropped the box of menus and raced toward her car.

The woman's back had been to the door, but Melanie saw that Jackson was still in her arms before she'd sprinted to her car and yanked open the door.

Now inside, she wept. She wanted to hit Rewind. Erase all of the happy moments she'd experienced the last several days. It was easier to go back into her shell. She'd be safe there, where no one could hurt her. She took notice of the time and placed the key into the ignition. She no longer needed a new outfit for tonight, but she wouldn't leave her aunt's friend waiting.

Melanie stared straight ahead, navigating the mountain curves. Thoughts of Rebecca filled her mind. She longed to call that sweet little girl her daughter, and to have her riding in the backseat of her car. It would probably never happen.

Up ahead, she spotted the sign for the boutique and hit the turn signal. The last thing in the world she wanted to do right now was shop. She'd do it for Aunt Phoebe.

Still numb from the shock of seeing Jackson with another woman, Melanie gripped the cold doorknob to the boutique and stepped inside. The air smelled of sweet strawberries.

A petite gray-haired woman dressed in a red suit and red flats scurried over, carrying an armful of clothes. "Welcome."

Melanie took notice of her name tag. "Hello, Estelle. I'm Melanie, Phoebe's niece."

She smiled wide. "Oh yes, I've been expecting you. I feel like I already know you. Phoebe's so proud of you."

Melanie's heart warmed. This town was smaller than she'd thought. Even the owner of the local dress shop knew her, or thought she did. Sweet little Estelle was clueless about the selfish decision she'd made that had cost her everything.

"I'm going to hang up these clothes that were left in the dressing room. Why don't you look around for a while, and then we'll find you the perfect outfit."

She couldn't find it in her heart to tell Estelle she didn't need a new outfit after all. "Thank you, Estelle. I'll be fine."

Ten minutes later, Estelle was fingering through a rack of dress pants while Melanie continued browsing the casual dresses. She caught the eye of a woman who quickly moved behind a mannequin displaying a black fur jacket. Melanie looked away and continued her search. Minutes later, she discreetly glanced in the woman's direction, and their eyes locked. Melanie's breath hitched. It was the odd woman from The Bean, and the one who'd shown up at Rebecca's school.

Anxious to escape the stranger's presence, Melanie snatched three dresses, all sheaths but in different colors, and headed to the dressing room. She turned at the sound of clicking heels behind her.

"Jackson loves women in red," the tall, dark-haired woman with wild curls said in a whisper.

Curls. It clicked. She was the woman Jackson was kissing earlier. She hadn't seen her face, but she recognized the raven hair. She tightened her grip on the hangers.

"Can't you speak?"

Melanie lifted a single brow. "Excuse me?"

The woman stepped closer. "I said Jackson loves a woman in red." She ran her hands down her dark leather pants. "You should go with the red dress."

Her skin chilled when the woman stepped into her personal space. Was that alcohol she smelled? This woman wasn't Jackson's type.

Melanie stepped back and bumped into one of the club chairs that lined the wall. She rubbed her leg and looked up. "Do I know you?"

Her face was stone. "I'm Rebecca's mother, Taylor." She shook her curls away from her face. "I thought it was about time I met the woman who's been spending so much time with my daughter."

Melanie's chin dipped. "Why are you here?"

Taylor placed her hand on her hip and pressed her thin lips together. "I've been here for a while. Jackson knows." She pulled a compact from her purse and admired her reflection. "He didn't tell you?"

Melanie's heart skipped a beat. Was Taylor the one who'd been calling obsessively? Why wouldn't Jackson mention she was back in town?

"So, I guess he didn't tell you," she said with a smirk. "I suppose he also didn't tell you we plan to reconcile." She reached out and yanked the red dress from Melanie's hand. "There's no need to try this on after all, is there?"

Her stomach rolled over. It wasn't possible. Jackson had told Melanie that Taylor had a drinking problem, and by the smell escaping the woman's mouth, that hadn't changed. There was no way Jackson would take her back. She'd abandoned her family.

"Are you okay? You look pale." Taylor draped a limp hand on Melanie's shoulder.

Melanie stumbled when she turned to make a quick escape into the dressing room. She slammed the door and turned the lock. At least behind the door, she wouldn't have to look at Taylor. Was Jackson still in love with her?

Following a knock on the dressing-room door, Taylor left with one last message. "Stay away from my daughter and my husband."

Her heels clicked and she was gone. "Ex-husband," Melanie said to her own reflection in the mirror and dropped to the floor and cried.

"You smell good, Daddy, like a Christmas tree."

Showered, shaved and dressed in khaki pants and a crisp white collared shirt, Jackson was nervous about his date with Melanie. After his conversation with the sheriff, his mind had eased about Taylor, and the excitement about spending an evening with Melanie returned, but so did the first-date jitters. "Thank you." Jackson glanced into the mirror. "Do you think my outfit is okay?"

Rebecca giggled and pounced up onto the bed. "Why does your outfit have to be okay? You're just going out to eat?" She nuzzled her face into Gigi.

"Well, I like Miss Melanie, and I want to look nice for her."

"I like her, too, Daddy." She flung herself back against the pillows and stared at the coffered ceiling. "Do you think she likes us?"

"Of course she does. Why wouldn't she?"

Rebecca placed her hands behind her head and wiggled her sock feet. "Well, Mary told me sometimes ladies don't like men who already have kids. They want their own kids, not somebody else's."

Jackson's stomach flinched. *Maybe they don't want a crazy ex-wife in the picture, either.* "I think Miss Melanie likes you just fine, so quit worrying, and don't believe everything your friends tell you."

"Where are you and Miss Melanie going?"

He poured a splash of aftershave into his hand and patted his cheeks. "We're going to the Italian place with the spaghetti and meatballs you like so much."

She jumped up and bounced on the bed. "The dark place?"

Jackson laughed. The restaurant wasn't exactly dark, but the lighting was set to create a romantic atmosphere. It was the main reason he'd decided to take Melanie there. Despite the unexpected arrival of Taylor, he hoped to plant the first seed in Melanie's head to move to Sweet Gum. "Yes, that's the place."

Rebecca jumped higher on the bed. "I want to go, too. I love that place!"

"Not tonight. Another time."

"Aw, man…you don't want me there so you can make goo-goo eyes at Miss Melanie."

This child was too much. He never knew what she was going to say. Jackson laughed and jumped onto the bed. He grabbed her around the waist and tickled her. "Yes, I do want to make goo-goo eyes at Miss Melanie."

Jackson's cell phone rang, and he ceased the tickle fest. He walked over to the dresser and grabbed the phone. He glanced at the caller ID and saw it was Melanie. Goose bumps rose on his arms. "Hello. I hope you've worked up a big appetite today."

Silence.

"Hello, Mel?"

"Uh, Jackson, I'm going to have to cancel tonight."

His shoulders slumped. He dragged his feet to his leather chair and flopped down. "What's wrong, Mel? You don't sound good. Is Phoebe okay?"

"Yes, she's fine. I have a migraine, that's all."

Jackson didn't believe it. Melanie's tone told him something was wrong, that it wasn't a headache. It was something more. "Come on, Mel—tell me the truth. I know that's not it." He stood up and paced in front of the chair. "What's up?"

As if on cue, the sound of pills rattling in a bottle echoed through the phone. "Nothing is up. I have a migraine. What time do you need me at The Bean tomorrow?"

Ready to end this call, he kicked his foot into the chair leg. "I can handle it. Why don't you take another day off?" He paused and eyed his daughter. "Look, I've got to get Rebecca some dinner."

"Goodbye, Jackson."

An abrupt click permeated the line. He never had a chance to say goodbye. Was it possible he'd moved too fast for her? Was this her way of slamming the brakes on the budding relationship? Had she gone back to her old ways, thinking he was too small-town for her?

He eased into his chair and gazed out the window. Two squirrels frolicked in the pile of leaves he'd raked yesterday. The swishing of Rebecca's corduroy pants filled the room when she walked toward him and climbed into his lap. The warmth of her hand on his cheek eased his disappointment. "What's wrong? You look sad."

He reached for her hand and gave it a gentle squeeze. "Miss Melanie had to cancel our date."

Rebecca pouted. "But you're all dressed and ready."

The sadness in her eyes tugged at his heart. "I know, but she's not feeling well." Refusing to wallow in his own disappointment, Jackson rose to his feet and lifted Rebecca over his head. "What do you say you and I go out for spaghetti and meatballs?"

She giggled and her legs flailed. "Like a date?"

He put her back on the ground. "Yes, exactly like a date, just you and me."

"Yes! I'm going to go put on my pink dress, the one with little daisies on it." She skipped out the door, leaving him alone with thoughts of Melanie.

When his cell phone rang, he jumped with hopes she'd changed her mind. He noticed the caller ID before he answered.

Unknown.

"This is Jackson," he snapped, knowing it was Taylor and expecting dead air. This time she stayed on the line. Muffled sounds came from the other end. "What do you want, Taylor?" he barked into the phone.

"I want to talk to my daughter," she slurred.

"You what?" Jackson's ears pounded.

"I want you to put my daughter on the phone, or I'm coming over to your house."

When he heard a loud clanking noise, Jackson knew Taylor had dropped the phone or passed out.

"Are you still there?" she asked.

Jackson shook his head. If he hadn't been so angry, he'd have felt sorry for her. "Yes, Taylor, I'm still here, but why don't you go to bed and sleep this one off?"

"I'm filing for custody of Rebecca." Her voice was garbled.

He stepped out into the hallway to keep an eye on Rebecca's door. He didn't want her to hear a word of this conversation. *If that's what you want to call it.* He lowered his voice. "You're what?"

Heavy breathing echoed through the line. "I'm going to file for custody, so expect the papers soon."

There was a click, and the line went dead. Jackson squeezed his eyes shut. *Lord, please, this can't be happening.*

Fuming, he stuffed his phone into his pocket and headed for the kitchen. He'd take care of Taylor on his own. No one needed to know about her return to the valley, especially Melanie. She had enough to deal with in her own life.

While Jackson waited for Rebecca to finish getting dressed, regret settled in. Why had he told Melanie he could handle things on his own at The Bean tomorrow? He missed her. A lot. Was this what it would be like when she returned to DC? He couldn't let that happen.

Rebecca walked into the kitchen dressed in her pink dress and patent leather shoes. Jackson smiled when he noticed the pink barrettes trying to pin down the crazy curls. "I'm ready," she announced.

"You look so pretty." He walked toward her and touched the barrettes. "I really like these."

"Thank you." She gazed up at Jackson. "Daddy, does Miss Melanie not like us anymore?"

Jackson took a seat at the kitchen table. "Sit down for a minute."

Rebecca plopped into the chair across from him.

"Of course she still likes us. She's just not feeling well."

She placed her elbows on the table and propped her fist underneath her chin. "I sure had fun baking cookies with her the other day."

His heart slowed. This was exactly what he'd feared the most. "What did you like the best about it?"

"Well... I liked it all, but the best part was when I pretended she was my mommy. I only pretended it for a minute, but it sure felt good." She tilted her head and fingered a curl.

Jackson was familiar with the feeling. He'd had it himself. The day he and Melanie played hooky, for a moment, as they sat by the river, he'd pretended she was his wife.

Chapter Fifteen

"Are you feeling better, dear?" Aunt Phoebe stood up from her corner desk in the kitchen and closed her Bible.

After a fitful night of sleep, Melanie decided it was time to get out of bed and face the facts. What she'd thought she and Jackson had was all a figment of her imagination. She inhaled the aroma of the freshly brewed coffee. "I'm feeling much better, but I could use some caffeine."

Aunt Phoebe's slippers scuffed along the floor. She placed the large steaming cup on the table.

Melanie wrapped both hands around the mug, and the warmth eased the chill in her bones. This was just what she needed. "Thanks." She didn't have the energy to explain what had transpired yesterday, so she remained silent.

Eventually she'd have to face Jackson. Feeling as she did the first time in the courtroom, she wanted to get it over with as soon as possible. But mostly, she needed to see Rebecca. She made everything seem better.

"Do you want me to cook you an omelet, or maybe some pancakes?"

With thoughts of Jackson and his ex-wife kissing, food was the last thing her stomach could handle. "No, thank you." She raised the mug. "This is all I need."

When the grandfather clock in the living room struck eight o'clock, Melanie got up from the table.

"Do you have to go so soon? I thought we'd have time to visit." Aunt Phoebe's eyes focused on the table.

She slipped back into her chair. Her stomach churned from the coffee. "I'm sorry. That was rude. It's just…" She turned to the window. The sun gleamed onto Aunt Phoebe's Bible on the desk across the room.

"What, dear?"

"Well, I wanted to see Rebecca." A hint of a smile took hold at the thought of seeing her.

Aunt Phoebe nodded. "She's a special little girl, isn't she?"

"Yes. I'm going to miss her when I go home."

A crooked grin formed on her lips. "What about Jackson? Won't you miss him?"

She flinched and jumped to her feet. "I don't want to talk about him." Her chair screeched across the floor.

A frown moved across Aunt Phoebe's brow. "I don't understand. You two seemed so happy spending time together."

Melanie slunk into her chair. A lump formed in her throat, and she swallowed hard. "So it wasn't just me? You saw it, too?"

"Of course I saw it. I don't understand why you're questioning the obvious."

"The obvious?"

"Yes, dear. You and Jackson have fallen in love."

Melanie's shoulders drooped. "You're half-right." She wiped a tear that slid down her cheek. "I have fallen in love with Jackson, but he's not in love with me."

"I've known that man his entire life. Since the day he rescued you, he's been happier than I've seen him in years."

Her words reminded Melanie of the kiss they'd shared in this very kitchen. So why had he kissed that other woman? She took a sip from her coffee and grimaced. It was cold.

"What makes you think he's not in love with you?"

"I don't think—I know. He and Taylor are reconciling." Hearing the words spoken made it all too real. Her decision had been made for her. She'd return to DC.

"Taylor? What on earth would make you think such a crazy thing?"

She wasn't sure which was worse, seeing Jackson and Taylor kissing inside The Bean, or the final blow, an attempt at reconciliation, straight from Taylor's mouth. Melanie pressed her fingers to her temples. "Taylor told me yesterday."

"Taylor's here, in Sweet Gum? Does Jackson know?"

Aunt Phoebe's softly spoken questions stabbed Melanie's heart. "Well, given the fact that I saw the two of them kissing, I'd say he knows."

"What?" Aunt Phoebe jumped from her chair, nearly knocking it over.

Melanie exhaled. "Please, sit down. I don't want to upset you… You're still recovering."

Phoebe placed her hand to her brow and took a seat. "Start from the beginning and tell me everything that happened."

After recalling each ghastly event that unfolded yesterday, Melanie felt sapped. It all seemed like a bad dream. She watched an expression of disbelief take hold of her aunt.

"I don't believe it. There has to be an explanation. I know Jackson, and he would never get back together with Taylor. Not only because of the pain he experienced as a result of her drinking, but especially since she abandoned her own child." She shook her head. "No way."

Maybe Aunt Phoebe was right. Perhaps there was an explanation, but the glimmer of hope faded. "How do you explain the kiss? I saw it with my own eyes."

"I can't, dear. Jackson will have to explain."

Melanie wasn't sure if she wanted to hear his explanation. "I'd better go get ready." Her voice was laced with disappointment and dread.

"Are you going to be okay?" her aunt asked in a whisper.

She turned to Aunt Phoebe. "Yes, I'll be fine."

Later, Melanie fumbled in her purse for her sunglasses, but realized she'd left them in Aunt Phoebe's kitchen. She pulled down the sun visor to shield her eyes from the blinding October sun that magnified the red and yellow leaves against a cloud-free sky. Soon the leaves would die and fall to the ground. Perhaps a sign it was time for her to return home. Despite the bright sunshine, a dark cloud appeared to hang overhead.

She glided her car into the empty parking spot next to Jackson's truck. Her heart gave a tug at the thought of her last ride in his vehicle, after a day at the orchard. How quickly things changed.

As Melanie reached for the doorknob, she spotted Rebecca sitting at the counter, reading a book. She smiled and turned the knob to enter The Bean, thrilled to see the one person who still brought her happiness.

The jingle of the bell caused Rebecca's head to turn with a jerk. She flew off the stool and darted toward Melanie. Her tennis shoes squeaked as they crossed the tile floor.

"Miss Melanie! I didn't think I'd ever see you again," she yelled.

The feeling of Rebecca's tiny arms around her waist nearly stole Melanie's breath. She released a forced laugh. "What would make you think such a thing?"

Rebecca's arms dropped, and her sad eyes looked up. "Since you broke your date with Daddy last night, I thought you didn't like us anymore."

Melanie flushed and turned toward Jackson, who stood behind the counter with his arms crossed. Turning her attention back to Rebecca, she cupped her chin. "Didn't he tell you I had a nasty headache last night?"

"Yeah." She looked down. "But I didn't know if it was true."

Melanie turned at the sound of Jackson's boots clomping across the floor.

"Of course it was true. Why else would Miss Melanie break our date?" Jackson said with a raised brow. "Speaking of a headache, I thought you planned to take the day off today to recuperate?"

She blew a wayward lock of hair away from her eyes and took off her jacket. "I had a good night of rest, and I feel better this morning." That couldn't have been further from the truth. She'd tossed and turned all night. Finally, around three in the morning, she moved to the Queen Anne chair and leafed through a quilting magazine for an hour.

"Since you still like us, does it mean you'll come with us to the apple festival tomorrow?" Rebecca asked and pressed the palms of her hands together. "Please."

Melanie couldn't imagine saying no and disappointing Rebecca, but the thought of spending the day with Jackson, given the circumstances, was wrong.

The jingle of the bell saved her from answering, at least for now. As a tour group stormed the restaurant, Melanie and Jackson went nonstop for the next hour.

By the time Rebecca was getting ready to board the bus, Jackson had barely spoken two words. Melanie was the one who should have been angry. Why was he acting mad?

Jackson wasn't prepared to see Melanie, at least not today. When she'd abruptly broken their date yesterday evening, his mind slipped back to his non-trusting ways, which was not a place he cared to be. But it was just as well. He had a full plate since Taylor was back in town. He needed to keep her away from Rebecca and figure out a way to get her out of town and out of their lives for good. "Have a good day at school. I'll pick you up at three o'clock."

"Can we go visit Sam later today?" Rebecca begged.

It wasn't a bad idea. Jackson wanted to find out when they could bring the dog home for good. He had a feeling that once Melanie left Rebecca would need Sam's companionship. "I think that's a great idea."

"Do you want to come, too, Miss Melanie?"

Jackson watched, and Melanie shook her head. His teeth clenched.

"No, I'm sorry, Rebecca. I need to be home with Aunt Phoebe."

Rebecca winced. "What about tomorrow? You'll come to the apple festival with us, won't you?"

His heart broke. Getting involved with a

woman who didn't live in the valley was a mistake. He had no idea what was going on in Melanie's head, and why the abrupt change of heart, but he couldn't let it continue. "Sweetheart, you heard Miss Melanie. She has to take care of Phoebe. It's why she's here. Now go on before the bus leaves without you."

She lowered her head and walked out the door. Outside in the parking lot, halfway to the bus, Rebecca dropped her book bag onto the asphalt and sprinted inside. With her arms once again around Melanie's waist, tears streamed down her cheeks. "I'll miss you, Miss Melanie." With a rapid turn, she was back out the door and boarded the bus.

Jackson hesitated, then shook his head.

"This is for the best, Jackson."

He jerked at the sound of her voice. "For the best… How can crushing a little girl's heart be for the best?" he snapped. "I thought you, of all people, would know about heartache, Mel."

"Rebecca needs a chance to know her real mother. I'm nothing but a stand-in." With her shoulders hunched, Melanie walked to the counter and flopped into the seat.

A car whizzed by outside, blaring its horn. Jackson took a seat next to Melanie. He placed his hand on top of hers. She flinched. "Where is all of this coming from, Mel? Please help me to understand what's going on in that head of yours, because right now, I don't have a clue what's happened to us."

She pulled her hand away and turned. With no concern for the tears racing down her face, her eyes held his gaze. "I saw you and Taylor kiss yesterday." She rubbed the back side of her hand across her cheek to erase the tears. "Aunt Phoebe asked me to drop off the new menus before I went shopping for a special outfit for our date. I wasn't spying on you." She looked away. "I saw you through the window when I walked up to the door."

The menus.

Jackson had found them at the front door when he'd left yesterday. He'd assumed the delivery truck had been in a hurry. When he thought of how he would feel if he saw Melanie kissing another man, his pulse accelerated. He wouldn't have liked it one bit. "Oh, Mel, please believe me—it's not what you think."

"You were kissing. What else am I supposed to conclude?"

He rubbed his hand across his chin. "She kissed me. She'd been drinking, and she came in demanding to see Rebecca." He decided not to mention the custody issue—he'd deal with it—but he had to make Melanie understand there was nothing going on between him and

Taylor. "Didn't you see me push her away?" He rested his hand on her back. "I don't want Taylor. You're the only woman I want to kiss, Mel."

Melanie ran her hands down the front of her jeans, once and then again. "No, I didn't see you pushing her away. I'm sorry I jumped to the wrong conclusion, Jackson, but that's not the only reason. Taylor *told* me you were reconciling."

His mouth dropped open. "You talked to her? When?"

"Yesterday, at Estelle's shop, I felt someone watching me. When our eyes met, I realized she was the odd woman who came into The Bean. Remember, the one who stared at Rebecca?"

He nodded. "Go on."

"She followed me back to the dressing room and told me you like women in red." Melanie paused and studied her fingernails. "When she said she'd been in town for a while and you knew, I couldn't understand why you hadn't told me. The only conclusion I came to was what she said was true. You two were reconciling, but you were afraid to tell me because you thought I'd change my mind and move Aunt Phoebe against her wishes."

His gut wrenched. After the time they'd spent together, the kiss they'd shared, everything he'd told her about Taylor and her destructive behavior, how could Melanie think that he'd do anything like that?

As though she read his mind, she reached for his hand. "I'm sorry I jumped to the wrong conclusion about you and Taylor. I should never have believed her. I know your heart, Jackson. You're a good man."

He moved in a little closer. "Good enough for you and Phoebe to join Rebecca and me at the festival tomorrow?" He tried not to get his hopes up, but he wanted her there as much as Rebecca did.

"Well, you'll just have to wait and see." She smiled and turned toward the kitchen, leaving behind an enticing floral scent.

No. He was wrong—he wanted her to come to the festival more than his daughter did.

At 2:00 p.m., Jackson dried the last plate as his thoughts centered on a future with Melanie. First he'd have to deal with Taylor.

As Melanie chatted away with the only customer in the restaurant, he slid his phone from his pocket. Sheriff Huggins had told him Taylor was staying at the Red Bird Inn, just outside of town. He'd programmed the number into his phone the other day, just in case. He wanted her out of his life, and he had the perfect plan.

The clerk answered on the first ring.

"Room ten, please."

The sound of a television blared through the line before anyone spoke.

"Taylor?"

"What do you want, Jackson?"

He cringed at the sound of her scratchy voice. He didn't believe Taylor wanted custody of Rebecca. Her motives were more than likely financial. He'd make her an offer she couldn't refuse. "I'm calling to let you know that I'm willing to pay you ten thousand dollars if you leave town today."

She gave a deep-throated laugh and coughed into the phone. "You can't buy me out of my daughter's life. I came here to see her, and I have every intention of doing so."

Jackson picked up the red dish towel and whipped it against the edge of the countertop. "You can't walk back into her life. She's a child. You'll confuse her."

"I think you're the one who's confused. She's my daughter. I have a right to see her. In fact— I'm going to her school now."

Click.

The line went silent. Jackson crammed his phone into his pocket and sprinted into the dining area. "Mel, we've got to close up. Now!"

With the last customer gone, Melanie was

busy clearing away the coffee cups. She turned with a jerk. "What's wrong, Jackson?"

"It's Taylor. She's going to Rebecca's school." He grabbed his coat and jammed his arms inside the sleeves. "Here, take your jacket." Jackson snatched the keys off the counter. "Let's go. I have to protect my daughter."

Jackson gripped the steering wheel and peeled out of the parking lot. "Put your seat belt on."

Melanie secured her belt. "How do you know Taylor's going to the school?"

"I called her. I wanted to pay her to leave town."

Several minutes later, Jackson tore into the school parking lot, practically on two wheels. Taylor had beat him. "There she is." He fumbled with his seat belt, his eyes peeled on Rebecca, Taylor and a teacher's aide, standing next to the swings.

He vaulted from the truck and raced to his daughter. Melanie followed. His heartbeat pummeled his eardrums when Rebecca turned to him and he saw her tears. He was too late, the damage done.

"Get away from my daughter." He snatched Rebecca into his arms, and adrenaline surged through his body. He looked at the young assistant. "Go get the principal."

Jackson watched the girl take off running toward the school. "It's okay. Daddy's here." He ran his hand through Rebecca's curls. Her body trembled.

Rebecca wiped away a tear and pointed toward Taylor. "That lady says she's my mommy." She sniffled. "She said I have to go live with her."

He lurched toward Taylor. "Leave! Now!"

Rebecca jumped and covered her eyes.

Melanie stepped toward Jackson and held out her arms. "Here, let me take her."

Without hesitation, Rebecca settled into Melanie's arms and nuzzled against her shoulder. "I want to go home, Miss Melanie."

Taylor approached them and pointed her finger in Melanie's face. Rebecca whimpered. "Just remember, I'm her mother. I always will be." She turned and hurried to the black Mustang parked along the curb. From the car, she yelled to Jackson. "You'll be hearing from my lawyer." She climbed into the car and zoomed out of sight.

Melanie turned to Jackson. "What's going on?"

He shook his head. "My worst nightmare has come true."

That evening, after following through with his promise to take Rebecca to see Sam, she was sound asleep in the back of Jackson's truck. Off in the distance, the call of a coyote caused Melanie to jump while she leaned against the outside of his vehicle.

"It's okay. He's just calling for his pack." Jackson zipped up his jacket. After the incident at the school, the three had headed to the Whitesides' house and had a nice visit with Sam. Rebecca hadn't mentioned the encounter with Taylor. Jackson was thankful. He needed time to figure out how to explain all of this to her.

They stood in silence for a few moments. Both looked up at the millions of stars congregating in the dark ink sky.

"Thanks for bringing me back to my car. I'm sorry about everything that happened today."

He shook his head. "This is like a bad dream. I can't believe Taylor came back after all this time. It's been four years and not a word from her. Why now?"

She shrugged. "Can I ask you something?"

Regret consumed him. He knew the question before she asked. "Sure."

Melanie sat down on the curb and motioned for Jackson to sit beside her. "Why didn't you tell me, or anyone, that Taylor wants custody of Rebecca?"

A pickup truck whizzed down the road. Its headlights pierced his eyes. He turned away and was face-to-face with Melanie. "You've got enough on your plate without dealing with my baggage." He released a sigh.

Her hand was warm when she placed it on his. "Jackson, you, of all people, know the importance of reaching out for help. You're fortunate enough to live in a town where people care about each other, but you're trying to be Superman and do it all on your own."

He playfully poked her in the rib cage. "Yeah, kind of like someone else I know."

"Who, me?" She arched her brow. "Seriously, Jackson, I'm a little hurt you didn't come to me when Taylor first came to town."

Jackson wondered the same thing, but deep down, he knew the reason. He was the rescuer. It had never been easy for him to allow others to help him. Even after Taylor first left him and Rebecca, he tried to handle everything on his own. "I'm sorry. The last thing in the world I'd ever want to do is hurt you."

She nodded. "I know that now." She squeezed his hand. "Listen, I want to help you. You're a wonderful father. No one loves Rebecca more than you do."

Jackson took a deep breath. "I don't think I'll ever forget the look on her face today." He dropped his head into his hands. "I can't lose her. She's my life."

"Let me help you, then."

He attempted a smile. "That's nice, but I'm not sure how you can."

Melanie sprang to her feet and placed her hands on her hips. "Come on. I'm a divorce attorney, or did you forget?"

Embarrassed, he stood. "Actually, I did forget." Taylor had turned his world upside down. He could hardly remember his own name.

"I deal with custody issues all of the time. Let me help you and Rebecca."

Jackson was touched by her offer, but with Phoebe getting stronger each day, it only made sense that Melanie would head back home to her job. He knew how the legal system worked. This could drag on for a long time. He couldn't expect her to put her life on hold to deal with his past baggage.

"Well, what do you say, Jackson? I can talk to my firm. Maybe they'll even let me handle the case pro bono." She winked.

Dread lingered, but he knew it was the right thing to do. "Thanks, but I'll take care of it."

Her shoulders slumped, and her smile faded. "Alright. Good night, Jackson." She turned, got inside her car and drove away.

Chapter Sixteen

Saturday morning, Melanie nibbled on an onion bagel while Aunt Phoebe drove for the first time since her stroke. Melanie slid her sunglasses on when the morning sunrise appeared over the mountainside.

"I don't know why the doctor made me wait so long to drive. I could have driven days ago." Aunt Phoebe rolled her eyes and took a sip of her steaming cinnamon latte.

The apple festival was the last place Melanie imagined she'd be headed to. Yesterday, she and Jackson had settled their misunderstanding about Taylor, and she became excited. But that soon waned after he refused her offer to help with his custody issue. Now her feelings were hurt, but her aunt had insisted she come.

It was an annual event, attracting people from all over the valley. Although she was nervous to face Jackson, she was anxious to see Rebecca. She needed a hug.

"Maybe I can talk some sense into Jackson. Why on earth he'd pass up an opportunity to have the best domestic-relations attorney on the East Coast represent him is beyond me." Aunt Phoebe crinkled her nose and yanked the sun visor down.

"Perhaps he doesn't trust me."

"Pfft… He's just being stubborn. Just give me a few minutes with him and I'll have him signing a retainer agreement."

Melanie chuckled. One thing her aunt wasn't short on was confidence in her ability of persuasion. "I hope you're right. I really want to help him, but last night he seemed resistant to the idea."

The festival was already in full swing by the time Aunt Phoebe zipped her tiny red sports car into the gravel parking lot. She had to hand it to her aunt—she did have style.

As they strolled past the booths filled with arts and crafts, Melanie turned at the sound of children giggling.

Her aunt locked arms with Melanie and pointed. "Look, there's Jackson and Rebecca—let's go."

"Hi," Jackson said as they approached.

"Do you have a minute to talk alone?" Melanie asked.

"Why don't I take Rebecca over to the hay-ride and give you two some privacy?" Phoebe offered.

A few minutes later, Melanie was alone with Jackson at her favorite spot by the river. She picked at the thread on the flannel blanket. "I wanted to apologize for last night. It wasn't my place to suggest I represent you."

A cool breeze ruffled some papers sticking out of Jackson's backpack lying on the corner of the blanket. He reached over and snatched the papers. "I was wrong, Mel. I need your help." He handed them to her. "When I went out to get the newspaper this morning, I was greeted by a process server. I guess Taylor wasn't joking. She had the papers drawn up several days ago."

After careful examination, Melanie turned to Jackson. "It's a petition for custody."

"Indeed it is."

"There's no way she'll get full custody. The facts are clear. She abandoned Rebecca and she has a serious drinking problem. Both of those work in your favor as an argument against granting her full custody."

He rubbed his brow. "What if the judge gives her visitation? I don't want Taylor playing any role in Rebecca's life."

"I understand your feelings toward Taylor, but she is Rebecca's biological mother. The court will take it into consideration." She paused and looked up at the woodpecker tapping on a nearby tree trunk. "If she agrees to get help, there's a chance the judge will grant visitation rights. You must be prepared for that."

With a determined look, his gaze traveled to Melanie, and her heart warmed. "Are you licensed in the state of Virginia?"

"Yes, I can practice law in Washington, DC, Virginia and Maryland. I'll call my partners today. I've been working on a few files already, since I wrapped up the kidnapping case, so I'm sure they won't have a problem with me staying to represent you."

"Miss Melanie!"

Rebecca ran toward the blanket, arms flailing. She squeezed in between Jackson and Melanie and handed her a purple coneflower. "I picked this special for you."

She accepted the flower and brought it to her nose. "Thank you. It's beautiful."

"I thought it was pretty, like you." Rebecca brushed her hair away from her eyes.

Aunt Phoebe approached the blanket. With the agility of a teenager, she flopped to the ground. "This child has more energy than a power plant. Now she wants to go through the corn maze." She reached into the cooler and popped the top of a Diet Coke. "I'll need a couple of these to keep up with her."

Melanie gave Rebecca's curl a tug. "How about I take you through the maze?"

Within a second, the child was on her feet and twirling. She spun faster and faster, then fell to the ground giggling. "But you're from the city. You'll get lost. You and Daddy better go together. He can hold your hand."

"The child's brilliant." Jackson threw a wink in Melanie's direction. "Why don't we all go through the maze?"

"Yay! I'll hold Phoebe's hand." Rebecca grinned.

Jackson reached for Rebecca and pulled her down onto his lap. "First, we need to talk about what happened yesterday."

Melanie's stomach lurched.

"You mean about the lady at school?"

"Rebecca, the lady told you the truth. She is your mother."

She tilted her head. "That's what she told me, but she didn't look like my mommy in the picture. I thought she'd look like those pretty singers I see on TV."

Melanie guessed the years of alcohol abuse had taken their toll on Taylor's appearance.

"She might not look the same, but she's your mommy," Jackson said in a whisper.

"She said I have to go live with her. Is that true?"

"No, you're not going to live with her." He looked at Melanie. "She just wants to spend some time with you, that's all."

How many times had Melanie witnessed the heartache of divorce? When children were involved, it was never easy. She hoped for Jackson and Rebecca's sake this case wouldn't turn their world upside down.

The tapping of Rebecca's Mary Janes echoed through the second-floor courthouse corridor. After three long weeks of waiting, today was the first scheduled court appearance. Long days at The Bean and late into the evening, Melanie had her nose stuck in law books. Jackson prayed it would pay off. He was ready to get this over with and move on with his life. A life that could only be lived with Melanie by his side—forever.

"Daddy, can you tell me again why we're here?" Rebecca tugged on his suit sleeve.

He stopped and led her to the bench that overlooked the first-floor lobby. Voices echoed from below. "We're here so the judge can decide if your mommy can see you."

"Why does he get to decide?"

Jackson wondered the same thing. How could one man or woman who'd never met either parent decide what was best for a child? Last night, he'd agreed with Melanie that it was best not to tell Rebecca the whole story. She believed there was no way a judge would grant Taylor full custody. He thought it was best to leave out the details. Why upset her this early in the game? "That's the law in Virginia."

"Can I tell the judge I don't want to see her?"

The last thing he wanted was for Rebecca to testify, but Melanie told him it could work in his favor. "You wouldn't be afraid?"

She shook her head, and her blond ponytails swung from side to side. "Nope."

He leaned over and took her into his arms. "You're a brave little girl."

They waited fifteen minutes for Melanie and Phoebe to arrive. Rebecca skipped up and down the hall when Jackson's phone chirped.

"This is Jackson."

"Hey, Jackson, it's Huggins."

Jackson wasn't sure why Sheriff Huggins was calling, but he sounded all business. A nerve twitched in his cheek. "Hey, what's up?"

"Where are you right now?"

"I'm at the courthouse for the custody hearing." This was a bad dream. "Rebecca and I are waiting for Melanie and Phoebe. It's supposed to start at two o'clock."

Silence traveled through the connection, and then the sheriff cleared his throat. "There's been an accident, Jackson."

Terror washed over him. The walls of the courthouse started to move closer, and the sound of Rebecca singing became garbled. *Melanie.* No, it couldn't be her. He'd already purchased the ring he planned to give her when he proposed, once this was all behind them. "What happened?" His voice shook.

"It's Taylor—she's dead."

"What? I don't understand."

"Her car went off Old Mill Road and straight into a tree. Judging from the skid marks, she must have been driving at least seventy miles per hour."

"Seventy miles…but that road is full of curves, and the speed limit is only thirty-five." Jackson squeezed his eyes shut. He wanted the custody issue resolved, but not this way.

"We found a bottle of alcohol in the car. My guess is she was heavily intoxicated. She'd have to be to drive at such a high speed."

Jackson ended the call and prayed. *Lord, please bless Taylor's family and help them through this difficult time.*

A few minutes later, Jackson looked up, and

there she was. Melanie, the love of his life. She was stunning. Dressed in a gray suit and carrying her briefcase, she was prepared to fight for him and Rebecca, but it was over before it began. He stood, exhaled a heavy breath and walked toward his future.

Melanie placed her briefcase at her feet. "Are you okay, Jackson? You look white as a snow owl."

He licked his lips and turned to Phoebe. "Can you take Rebecca down to the cafeteria? I need to speak with Mel."

As Phoebe took Rebecca's hand and directed her toward the cafeteria, Melanie's eyes were wide. "What's going on?"

They took a seat on the same bench where he'd heard the news only moments earlier. As he explained to Melanie about the speed and the alcohol, and in the end, a deadly crash, she gave a shaky nod.

He took her hand. It felt moist. "Taylor's death is just another reminder of how precious life is and how quickly it passes you by." He took a steadying breath. "Marry me, Mel, this spring, at your favorite spot by the river."

He reached into his coat pocket and felt the small velvet box. In one swift move, it was in his hand and he was down on one knee, in front of the love of his life, the woman he wanted to build a life with.

When he looked up, she dropped her gaze to him. A stream of tears streaked her face.

"Last night—"

She paused, and Jackson's breath caught in his throat. Jackson reached for her left hand. "What about last night?" he asked, confused.

She dipped her chin. "I dreamed of our wedding last night—it was by the river."

His eyes closed for a moment to thank God for this woman. "I love you, Mel... Let me make that dream come true."

"I love you, too, Jackson Daughtry. Since the day of my accident, you've never stopped coming to my rescue."

Jackson opened the box and pulled out the ring. "Does that mean yes?"

She cupped his face in her hands and pressed her lips to his. "Yes. There's nothing I want more than to share my life with you and Rebecca."

His heart soared as he slid the ring onto her finger. Jackson sprang to his feet and scooped his fiancée into his arms. And there, in the middle of the hall at the Sweet Gum courthouse, the newly engaged couple twirled, just like Rebecca.

Epilogue

Six months later

Rebecca squinted when she looked up into the late-May sunshine. "Are you really my mommy now, Miss Melanie?" The black-capped chickadees chirped and flitted from limb to limb in the nearby dogwoods. The sweet fragrance of lilac filled the air. It was the perfect day for a wedding.

"Yes, she is, Squirt. We're married now, so you can call her Mommy, not Miss Melanie." Jackson, handsome as ever dressed in his dark tuxedo, scooped his daughter into his arms and smothered her with kisses.

"Daddy, you're wrinkling my dress." Rebecca giggled.

Tears pressed against Melanie's eyes while she watched her family. Her aunt Phoebe was right. God did have a plan for her life. Not only did He plan for Jackson to rescue her after her accident, but also He planned to give her a family once again. She could hardly contain her joy. "Yes, Jackson, put her down. I'm dying to see her twirl in that beautiful dress."

The second Jackson put Rebecca on the ground, her arms extended and she started to twirl. She spun like a top. Giggles filled the air, and a gentle breeze caught the bottom of her tea-length champagne lace dress. She stopped with a halt and looked at Jackson and Melanie. "This is the best day ever."

When Jackson rested his strong hands on his bride's waist, she caught a whiff of his spicy cologne. "Ah...you smell like the outdoors."

He laughed and gave her a playful squeeze. "So that's why you wanted to get married out here, because the smell reminds you of me."

When Jackson suggested they have an outdoor wedding by the river, she couldn't think of a better place. He knew, after the day he brought her to the orchard to go apple picking, it had become her favorite spot in Sweet Gum Valley. "Well, yes, but there's another reason I wanted to get married here, Jackson."

He nuzzled his lips on the back of her neck. "Really? Do tell."

"This is where I first realized I loved you."

She turned to face him, and their eyes locked. "It was the day you brought me here on a picnic."

"I thought it was Phoebe's brownies you fell in love with that day." He winked and gave her waist a tickle.

"What about my brownies?" Aunt Phoebe asked as she walked toward them, holding hands with Dr. Roberts.

Once Aunt Phoebe returned home after her rehabilitation, Melanie realized Jackson had done a little matchmaking. Dr. Roberts became a regular guest for Sunday dinner. He said her fried chicken was the reason he kept coming back, but Melanie knew otherwise. He and Aunt Phoebe had a standing date at the movies every Saturday night. Melanie was thrilled to see her aunt so happy. Who knew? Maybe there'd be another wedding in the near future. She smiled at the thought.

"Congratulations, you two. I knew the day of Melanie's accident this boy was smitten." Dr. Roberts patted Jackson on the back.

Jackson's face reddened. "Was I that obvious?" His smile was tender when he glanced at Melanie.

Dr. Roberts extended his hand to Melanie. "So, Melanie, I'm curious. What made you change your mind about moving Phoebe to DC, and staying in the valley yourself?"

Melanie remembered the exact moment when she knew she'd never return to DC. Aunt Phoebe belonged in Sweet Gum, and so did she. She looked around at all the faces of the people who'd come to celebrate their wedding day. Even Dr. Roberts's granddaughter, who'd just graduated from college, came for the special day. Melanie knew in her heart that she was home. She turned to Dr. Roberts. "It was the day I came into work at The Bean and the stove had broken. Half of the town had come out to help, and no one expected anything in return."

A smile tugged at her lips. "I never knew people could be so caring and unselfish toward their neighbors. It just isn't that way in DC. I knew then it was wrong for me to take Aunt Phoebe away from the people she loved so much, and who loved her." She ran her hands down the front of her beaded gown and took in this picturesque spot, her special place by the river. Now it would always be her and Jackson's special place. She wrapped her arms around Jackson's waist, drawing him against her. "Plus, I couldn't take her away and risk never seeing this gorgeous man again."

Jackson released a loud breath. "Well, I'm glad I was at least part of the reason you decided to stay." He kissed Melanie's cheek and winked at Phoebe.

Melanie wanted to keep the other reason between her and God. Their first outing, when Jackson brought her to this magnificent clearing by the river, she felt God's presence for the first time since the accident. She knew then that God had brought Jackson and his daughter into her life. It was all part of His plan. He was offering her a second chance at happiness. When Jackson had dropped to his knee in the middle of the courthouse and proposed, she knew she'd finally captured her dream.

* * * * *

If you enjoyed SECOND CHANCE ROMANCE,
*look for these other emotionally gripping
and wonderful stories*

THE RANCHER'S TEXAS MATCH
by Brenda Minton

LONE STAR DAD
by Linda Goodnight

A FAMILY FOR THE FARMER
by Laurel Blount

Available now from Love Inspired!

*Find more great reads at
www.LoveInspired.com*

Dear Reader,

Growing up in the suburbs of Washington, DC, one of my favorite areas was the Shenandoah Valley. The beauty of the valley was prevalent year-round, but autumn was always my favorite time to visit. The magnificent colors painted on the Blue Ridge Mountains were a constant reminder of God's presence in my life.

In 2015, when I heard about Harlequin's Blurb to Book competition, I knew this was my opportunity to complete a project I started in 2010 but never finished. Like Melanie, who dreamed of having a family once again, my dream was to write a book.

God created us to have goals and dreams. The funny thing was, my dream was to write a book, but I never dreamed of having it published. That's what makes our God such an awesome God. He took my little dream and turned it into a magnificent gift just for me.

I encourage you all to have dreams; God is listening and He knows your heart.

I love to hear from readers. You can email me at authorjillweatherholt@gmail.com or follow my blog at jillweatherholt.com. I'm also a contributor at inspyromance.com.

Blessings,
Jill Weatherholt